A LONELY DEATH

The scene was silent and motionless, even as Monte moved his gaze in closer and saw Weaver sitting by the fire pit.

The riders moved closer, their horses making soft thuds on the ground. They dismounted at about a hundred feet out, and getting no answer to their call, they walked on in. Monte could see Weaver's hat pushed forward, almost meeting with the bushy blond mustache. The hat brim had snow on it, as did Weaver's overcoat and the saddle he leaned against.

Monte and Johnny stopped a few feet from the body. Johnny leaned over and picked up the whiskey bottle, which, with the snow shaken off, proved to be empty.

Johnny looked at Monte. "Must have had too much of this and fell asleep. Froze to death." He dropped the bottle on the ground.

Monte grimaced. "Not unless he had another bottle of it. It wouldn't have lasted him that long."

Johnny handed his reins to Monte and squatted at Weaver's side. He opened the coat and closed it back up, then looked upward at Monte. "He's been shot, all right. Square in the chest."

North of Cheyenne

John D. Nesbitt

LEISURE BOOKS   NEW YORK CITY

A LEISURE BOOK®

October 2000

Published by

Dorchester Publishing Co., Inc.
276 Fifth Avenue
New York, NY 10001

ISBN 0-8439-4783-7

The name "Leisure Books" and the stylized "L" with design are trademarks of Dorchester Publishing Co., Inc.

Printed in the United States of America.

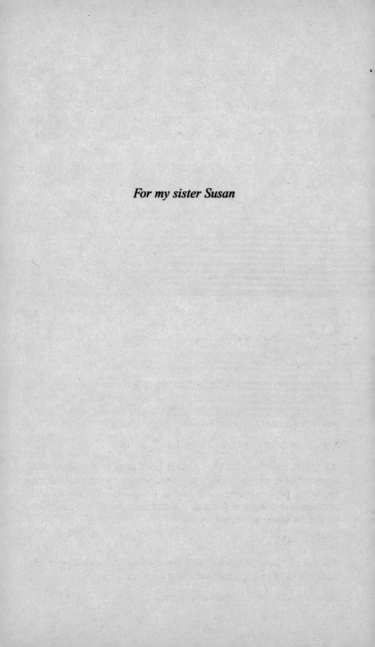

For my sister Susan

North of Cheyenne

Chapter One

A cold wind blew from the north. Monte Casteel rode with his head canted so that the wind would press down on his hat brim rather than lift it. It wasn't a hard, driving wind, but if it caught the underside it was enough to carry away a hat. Even if a man thought there was no one within miles, there were things he didn't do if he didn't have to. One was grab the saddle horn, and another was hold on to his hat. Both his hands had better uses; his left hand held the reins, and his right hand was free for any need that came up, like leading another animal, shaking out a rope, or drawing a gun. Holding on to his hat gave a rider bad balance, while keeping a hand free gave him good balance. So even if a lowered hat brim cut off some of his field of vision, Monte Casteel rode that way because it was good principle.

With his downward view he saw the tawny coat and dark mane of his buckskin horse, the muscles shifting as the horse walked onward into the wind. Monte saw his own left hand, in a leather riding glove darker than tanned deerskin, where it held the reins in front of the saddle horn. The sleeve of his sheepskin coat, darker yet but still a yellowish tan, met the glove and overlapped it. Farther down he saw the leg of his dark gray wool pants against the brown saddle leather.

In normal weather he would scan the country every minute or so, as any rider would, but with the cold wind he kept his head down. From time to time he lifted his head in a rolling slant to keep the surface of the hat against the wind, and in that way he took a glance at the country. If he needed a longer look, he raised his right hand and touched it to his hat for a moment. He did so now, for as he looked at the rolling plains country ahead, he saw three men on horseback.

The wind had died down since midday, but it was still cold enough to make the eyes water. Monte blinked and took a good look. The three horsemen had come to a stop and were waiting for him ahead on the trail. He felt for his gun beneath his coat, then touched his spurs to the buckskin and moved on, looking up every minute or so to see that the men were still waiting.

A man didn't ask personal questions in the West, but anyone out on the open country had a right to ask where a traveler was headed. It was considered poor manners, if not downright suspicious, to pull off the trail to avoid a meeting. Monte had nothing to hide, and even though he didn't like the feeling he had about the three men up ahead, he rode on. For the last fifty yards he kept his gaze right on the men, who were watching him approach.

The men sat three abreast on the right side of the trail, with their backs and their horses' rumps into the wind. All three had their heads cocked up and back against the dying wind, and Monte could see they all had their hands on their saddle horns. Monte kept his hands in sight, too, and as he brought his horse to a stop he touched his right hand to his hat brim.

"Good afternoon," he said.

The man in the middle answered. "Good afternoon." The man's head moved, perhaps in response to the wind on his hat, and then the voice came again. "Name's Elswick."

Monte took a long glance at the man who spoke. He wore a dark hat with a tall, narrow crown dented on each side. The face had lean features, with a dark mustache clipped neatly above the upper lip. He wore a dark wool coat, a little heavier than a southern frock coat. Beneath the coat he wore a dark vest, buttoned, with a silver watch chain. To set off his neatness he wore a pair of dark leather riding gloves. Monte guessed him to be in his middle thirties.

"My name's Casteel. Monte Casteel."

Elswick nodded, then tipped his head to the left. "This is my hired man, Mr. Thrall."

Monte looked at the man being introduced, who sat with a dull look on his face. The man was blocky and primitive-looking, although he was probably still in his twenties. He wore a drab hat with a low crown and narrow brim. Bristly brown hair stuck out beneath the hat, and a pair of blue-gray eyes squinted out from beneath a heavy brow. He face carried no mustache but rather a thick stubble, also brown, that showed he hadn't shaved in a few days. He had an upturned nose and a short neck, and his upper body ran thick in the chest and shoulders. Beneath a brown sack coat he wore a heavy gray flannel shirt with no vest; sticking out from the sleeves of the coat, his hands showed red and meaty. The man named Thrall bobbed his head in recognition.

Monte nodded back. "Pleased to meet you."

Thrall answered in a gravelly voice, "Likewise."

Elswick then turned to his right, and in a voice that sounded clear and sharp in contrast with that of his hired man, he said, "This is Mr. Pool. He works for me too."

Monte looked at the third man, who had seemed out of place even at the first quick glance. He wore a black hat with a wide brim and undented crown, and his long, dark, wavy hair was tucked behind his ears and hanging in strands on the nape of his neck. He had a lean, narrow build, so that his black wool coat, black vest, and white shirt hung loosely upon him. Only his black gloves fit closely. He had dark, narrow-set eyes that flickered as Monte looked at him. All of his face was thin—a narrow nose, a pointed chin, a thin neck, and a sparse beard that, like Thrall's, probably felt the razor once a week. He had a sallow complexion, as if the sun had shined on his face in a different climate.

"Pleased to meet you," Monte said.

Pool's mouth opened to show a set of narrow teeth, gapped in front, but he did not speak.

Monte felt the discomfort hanging in the air, and as he turned to look again at Elswick, a gust of wind came up. Pool's hat flew off, and all four horses lurched. Then everything settled down.

"Go ahead and get it," Elswick said, glancing at Thrall.

Thrall's head bobbed, and he swung down from the saddle. His horse had turned a little in the commotion, so that Thrall, when he dismounted, had the horse between him and Monte. It was a patently discourteous move in the company of a stranger, and Monte wondered if the man might come up with a gun. But he didn't. He came around in front of his horse, reins in his thick right hand, and stooped to pick up Pool's hat.

As Thrall stood up with the hat, Monte saw a gun and holster beneath the sack coat, on the right side. He could tell Thrall wasn't much of a gunman if he kept his right hand tied up by holding the reins.

Monte now looked at Pool, who waited for his hat. Monte noticed the receding hair, the dark stunted forelock, and the pale forehead and scalp, all of which went out of sight as Pool took the hat in his gloved right hand and jammed it onto his head. As nearly as Monte could tell, Pool had not said so much as thanks, for no sound came out of the exchange.

As Thrall pushed his horse backward into position next to Elswick, Monte looked again at Pool. He saw that the man wore large-roweled spurs and had tapaderos on his stirrups. Everything about him made him seem like an outsider.

Monte looked back at Thrall, who again had his horse blocking him from view until he grabbed the pommel and pulled himself up into the saddle.

Monte's gaze went back to Elswick, who spoke in a sharp voice.

"Where you comin' from?"

Monte felt himself being taken aback. As he heard the first couple of words he expected the standard question of where he was headed, so the rest of the question came as a surprise. Perhaps it was intended to be that way.

"Down by Cheyenne," he said. "I just finished the season on the MT Ranch, northwest of Cheyenne about twenty miles."

"Never heard of it," said Elswick, shaking his head.

Monte felt a spark of resentment at what seemed to be a challenge; then he realized Elswick might be trying to raise such a spark. "I hadn't either," he said, "till someone mentioned it to me."

Elswick, as if not recognizing the answer, asked, "Where you headed?"

"North and further west, I suppose. I thought I'd like to see the mountains before we get into deep winter."

"Uh-huh. It's better country over there. And the work's all done around here."

Monte nodded. "I imagine just about everyone's done with fall roundup and shipping."

"Well, there's no work here." Elswick had his head back again, as if into the wind.

Monte turned down the corners of his mouth. "Well, I wasn't really askin' for work. Are you the foreman of a ranch hereabouts?"

Elswick sniffed at his left mustache. "I'm the owner." He paused and then added, "We've had a little trouble here."

Monte raised his eyebrows. "Local trouble?"

"Let's just say it's some people locally as well as some newcomers."

Monte shrugged. "I just got here myself, and I hope it's no offense if I'm passin' through." He looked around. "Most of this is open range anyway, isn't it?"

Elswick seemed to be looking down his nose as he said, "In point of fact, this is my land we're on right now."

Monte pushed out his lower lip and then said, "No harm in my crossin' it, I hope."

"No, not as long as you keep moving." Elswick straightened himself in the saddle, and as he did so he moved his coat and showed a pistol butt and holster on his right hip.

"Uh-huh," Monte answered, aware of his own gun beneath his coat. "That was my plan to begin with."

"Good enough," said Elswick, with less of the threatening tone in his voice. "About an hour's ride to the north here, you'll find a little town called Eagle Spring. It's not much account, but the trail goes right through it."

"Thanks," Monte answered. "I suppose I'll move along." He touched his hat brim and looked at each of the men as he said, "Pleasure meeting you all."

"Same here," Elswick answered.

"Likewise," came the gravelly voice of the hired man Thrall.

Pool said nothing. He had taken out a long-bladed jackknife and a plug of tobacco, and he was cutting off a slice into his open mouth. The narrow teeth looked yellow in contrast with the black gloves.

Monte nudged the buckskin and rode on, not looking back until he had ridden for more than a mile. When he stopped the horse and turned it, he saw no trace of the three men he had just met.

Riding on, he felt nagged by the meeting. He had not liked any of the three men, for each in his own way had been disagreeable, but mostly he had not liked Elswick. The man was imperious, condescending. Even the tone in which he had said he had never heard of the MT had been close to insult, as if he was implying there might be untruth to something if he hadn't heard of it. Monte did not like being told to move along, not out here in the free country, where very little of the land was privately owned. If Elswick was like most cattlemen, he held title to the land where he had his ranch headquarters and to a few other claims that had water holes or bordered on a stream. And even if he did own the land he didn't need to take such a high-handed tone, much less show his hardware.

Moreover, Monte didn't like Elswick for the kind of men he hired and the way in which he treated them. Thrall was like a dog, trained to do the dirty work, while Pool looked like he fit the pattern of the hired gun, probably brought up from somewhere down south. Pool was the worst, he thought—the type of man who did what he was paid to do without asking questions—but Elswick couldn't be much better if he paid a man like that.

Monte shook his head. Maybe he would never see any of them again, but he knew that if he did, it would not be in friendship.

The wind had died down to a breeze, still cold but not as sharp as before. Monte rode on, trying to put the men out of his mind as he looked at the country around him. It was rolling plains country, not as flat as the grasslands that sloped away to the east, and not as hilly as the land to the west as it reached up to the mountains. The rangeland had already seen a month of frost and one good snowstorm, so it lay in the autumn colors of gray and tan. Contrary to what Elswick had said, it was good grass country. Off to either side, Monte saw cattle in the distance—dark spots in the afternoon sunlight. Of course, this was good grass country, as anyone could see. The cattle knew it, just as the buffalo had known it for years before them. If the country was that much better off to the west, he thought, what was Elswick doing out here?

Monte took another broad look at the landscape. It was pure and clear for miles in every direction. He could not see a building or a fence, although he knew he would see both again before long. And somewhere up the trail was Eagle Spring, a town that didn't come highly recommended—or, considering who had made the remark, maybe it wasn't so bad, as far as towns went.

*　*　*

The sun was slipping toward the western mountains when Monte rode into Eagle Spring. The wind had died down, but the air was beginning to chill on its own, and he thought it would be a good idea to put up for the night. He had slept out in the open so many times that a livery stable seemed plenty comfortable, and he liked to be near his horse when he was this far from anyone he knew.

The town had little to distinguish it from other frontier towns. It was laid out square, with its length running north and south. The main street, wide and already dished out in the middle, was flanked on either side by frame buildings. The lumber was weathered, but nothing looked old yet, and the tallest trees were shorter than any of the buildings.

Seeing two freight wagons and a pack outfit, he imagined the town saw a few travelers. He supposed they came this way for the same reason he did, to take a shortcut from the main road that went north and then west. The trail he had followed during the day had been more than a one-horse trail, and he doubted even further that Elswick had any right to tell someone to move along.

Up ahead on his left he saw a building that looked like a livery stable, with large doors and a tall front. A man in bib overalls was hooking up a four-horse team to a ranch wagon that had a tarpaulin tied down over a load. Monte slacked his reins another half inch and let the horse keep walking. He looked at either side of the street now, taking in the few details to be seen, when all of a sudden he saw a form that gave him a jolt.

It was a woman, a shapely woman in a wool dress and matching hat, with a full head of blond hair reaching from the hat to the collar. His whole body had reacted before he had consciously seen and thought. It had happened before, at least a dozen times—a flash of blond hair, or the turn of a figure—and always it had been a false alarm. This time it wasn't. She was walking along the board sidewalk on his right, going the same way and a little ahead of him. The horse was walking faster than she was, so Monte was able to catch up until he could see her face and then her profile. As he took a full look, he was sure it was the woman whose golden image had never left him.

Monte shook the reins, and the horse pulled ahead of the woman. After a few quick steps, Monte turned the horse in and swung down. Still holding the reins, he stepped up close to the sidewalk and spoke her name.

"Dora."

She stopped. A blank look crossed her face, followed by a flicker of recognition. "You haven't changed," she said. "I'd know you anywhere."

Monte's mouth felt dry as he said, "Who'd have thought it would've been here?"

She arched her brows. "I suppose it seems normal enough to me. I live here."

Monte hesitated and then started a question. "With—?"

"No," she said in a low voice as she gave a slight shake to her head.

Monte looked around, sensing that she didn't want to speak out loud in public about a man she was no longer with. Monte dropped the reins, and the horse moved back a couple of steps and hung his head as he had been trained to do. Monte stepped up on to the sidewalk, his heart beating faster.

"Then he's gone?"

Her brows drew together as she said, "I left him. I had to. I discovered things about him that—well, let's just say it was a shame to me in public as well as in private."

As she spoke, Monte took a glance at her. She hadn't changed, either. She was still slender and shapely. The gray wool dress did not bulge in front or on the sides, and her white cuffs and lace collar looked as fresh as ever. Her face was still smooth and white, without a wrinkle, and her wide, blue eyes and full red lips still looked like a girl's.

"Are you done with him, then?"

"Oh, yes. Long ago." She looked around and then continued in a soft voice. "I was able to get the marriage annulled. Then I went back to Cheyenne, where I met my present husband."

Monte felt his heart sink as he glanced around. "Then you live with him here?"

"Yes," she answered, her voice a little louder now. "With him and our daughter."

Monte looked along the street at the buildings and then back at her. He felt he didn't have much time, standing on the edge of the sidewalk with his horse ground-hitched in the street, so he asked, "What does he do? Does he have a business?"

"He has a ranch. His name is Carson Lurie."

That figured. A cattleman who wanted to be

someone and had connections in Cheyenne. This fellow was probably a member of the Cheyenne Club and moved in those circles. That was how she would have met him. Monte nodded.

Dora's voice was lower as she spoke again. "I came to him clean. I tried not to carry anything over from that earlier period."

Monte looked at her without answering. She had a serious but not stern look on her face, and from the smoothness of her speech he imagined she had made up her mind and rehearsed her lines a while back.

"I'd like to keep it that way," she said, her face now softening in a wince.

He felt it was as close as she would come to any earlier tenderness, and he thought he understood why. She was trying to make over her life. She would feel she needed some control over how much of the past to let in, even with him. She was count-ing on his friendship and was asking him not to say anything. He didn't know if coming to her husband "clean" meant that she hadn't mentioned her for-mer marriage, or that she hadn't mentioned the other man's disgrace, or that she had told her pres-ent husband at least the bare details and then had burned her ships. Whatever the case, he sensed that she was asking him not to go out of his way to say what he might know.

"That's all right," he said. "You won't have to worry about me." He held out his hand, still in its leather glove.

She held out hers, small and slender in a dark

blue wool glove, and their hands pressed for an instant.

"Thank you," she said. "And it's good to see you again."

"It's good to see you, Dora," he said as his hand came away. He backed off the sidewalk and tipped his hat. "So long."

"Good-bye," she said as she walked away.

As Monte moved to the horse he put his right hand on the reins beneath the bit, and with his left hand he drew the reins up from the ground. He realized she had not spoken his name, nor had she asked him if he was staying or passing through. He moved his head to either side. It didn't matter. She had been direct and had gone to the part that concerned her. That was all right with him. If he thought he knew something, that was her business and not his. If anything, he was glad to know she wasn't with Pryor anymore, but as for his knowing it in Eagle Spring, it was nothing to feel either good or bad about.

Monte looked up and around before leading the horse out into the street. As he did so, he saw another familiar figure. Elswick was putting his horse into motion and turning away to the left. He had apparently stopped long enough to see the end of the conversation, then turned away to avoid exchanging glances.

Monte felt a spark of resentment again. He'd stay where he damn well pleased, and for as long as he pleased. He led the buckskin horse out into the street and headed for the livery stable.

Chapter Two

Monte lay back on the bed he had rolled out on the straw. It was still warm in the stable, and the comforting smell of hay, straw, and horses surrounded him. In a little while he would wash up and go look for something to eat, but for the time being he had taken off his gun and boots so he could relax.

The meeting with Dora had stirred things up inside him, and not in a way that left him with a pleasant afterglow. It had kicked loose some old memories—images that came attached with feelings of an earlier time. The sensation was so strong that he almost felt as if he were living in that era, but the straw bed, the smells of the stable, and the fading light at the open door kept him conscious that he was in Eagle Spring, Wyoming, on a fall afternoon slipping into evening.

He had known her when they were growing up

in Cheyenne, when his father worked in a livery stable quite a bit larger than this one. Her father worked in the land office. When she was ten, her father died. A year later, her mother married a banker. Monte knew her as a pretty girl with blond hair, a girl just a couple of years younger than he was, and then a sad girl who had lost her father. Later it would seem that they were closest in that year between her father's death and her mother's remarriage, when she looked to Monte for friendship and comfort. After that, life in the banker's house seemed to change her, as she then took music lessons and began to have her clothes made by a seamstress.

When Monte was fourteen his mother died, and when he was sixteen his father died. He was alone then, more than ever before. He was still friends with Dora and could still visit her, but by then he could see they were growing apart. She was at a place in her life where she could not fill the emptiness in his, even through friendship; and his feelings for her just deepened in his loneliness. Left to his own young hopes and fears, he adored her beyond reason. She seemed to stand for everything he had lost and everything he ever hoped to have.

He went to work at ranch work, on one place and then another. His long hours were filled with thoughts of a golden-haired girl—a girl he once hoped would be his but that he now feared would never be. She seemed to be present in every long winter ride, in every bunkhouse, at every campfire. When he saw a deer, or a den of cub foxes, or a hawk soaring in the sky, he thought of her. When he rode a gentle horse, it seemed as if she was in the air along with them. Of course, she had been in all those places, he realized later, because in his adoration he had put her there.

Still he saw her from time to time, as his hope grew into despair. He knew she would end up with some fellow in a starched collar, a tie and stickpin, and a top hat. That was the type of man he saw around her, or with her, when his path crossed hers in Cheyenne.

Then she met a slick jasper from St. Louis, a man who came out to make it big in mining. His name was Ralph Pryor. Monte still had a clear picture of him—well-groomed, clean-shaven, with one brown eye and one blue eye. He had talked down to Monte the one time they had met, as if Monte had come to collect for the ice or coal. Monte remembered seeing him another time, when Pryor was coming out of a brothel during his engagement to Dora.

Monte begged her not to marry the man, for her own sake and not his, he said, although he knew he could not separate the two. "Even if you never speak to me again," he pleaded, "don't do it."

But she did. Before she turned twenty she had married Ralph Pryor and had gone off with him to Colorado. Although there was some relief now in knowing she had not stayed with him, there was little satisfaction in being able to say he had told her so. Nor was there much pleasure in knowing that Pryor had panned out the way he had.

Mining and ranching were two different ways of life, almost two separate worlds. Monte didn't know much about mining, but he imagined there were ways of losing face other than just losing a big investment. Pryor must have done something bad that Monte could only imagine by comparison.

When a cowpuncher went broke, it was no disgrace. He was usually between jobs if he went broke, so he just moved on until he found another job. But if things really went to hell on him—usually through some bad deed connected with drinking, or not paying his debts, or going back on his word, or making light with something that pertained to another man—he lost his respect and had to leave the country.

That must have been the way it was with Pryor. He must have played it out too far, and then there was nothing left. Monte grimaced. Maybe it hadn't caused him personal shame to do whatever had brought him to the end of his rope, but it must have been hard to look in the mirror after a woman like Dora had walked out of his life for good. Even a fellow like Pryor would have to feel it.

Well, it was their life, he thought. He'd had his own ups and downs, such as they were, and he doubted she had ever worried much about him in the past eight years.

After she had gone off with Pryor, Monte had told himself he wanted to see the world. He went south to work with a drover he met in Cheyenne, and for the next two seasons he trailed cattle north from Texas to Montana. After that he found work in the southwest, across west Texas and eastern New Mexico, still telling himself he wanted to see more, to see what life was like in a warmer climate. Eventually he found out that life wasn't any better in one place than another, so he went back to the country that was in his blood—the northern ranges. He didn't ask about Dora, and he never heard anything about her. For all he knew now, he may have been in town when she was back in circulation. But it wouldn't have mattered.

Monte let out a sigh. It had been a long time, and he couldn't say things had gotten a great deal better. It seemed as if he had been carrying around something he hadn't wanted to let go but ought to. Meeting her today had brought back old, raw feelings and had shown him that things still were not really over.

He looked at his stockinged feet, at the buckskin horse, and then at the open doorway. It was still daylight. He leaned over and drew his ditty bag toward him. Opening the drawstring, he took out a small bundle wrapped in cotton cloth. Even wrapped up, it was barely larger than a pocket watch. He unfolded the cloth and looked at the token that lay in his palm.

It was a piece of scrimshaw, or whale ivory, as he had been told when he bought it. It was a wide oval, about an inch and a half wide and an inch tall, pale yellowish-white with a dark etching of three roses. The flowers lay horizontally with long stems.

More than once he had imagined a whaler, far from home and his sweetheart, engraving the image. It was a pleasant thought, but he also knew that the artisan could just as likely have been sitting in a seafront shop with a scolding wife at his ear. The lonesome whaler, the cowboy of the seas, made a better story, though.

Monte smiled as he gazed at the token. It was just as pretty as it had been the last time he had looked at it—or the first time, when he saw it in a shop in Santa Fe. He had bought it thinking he might some-day meet a woman to give it to. He had probably never given up on the idea of giving it to Dora, but now he knew it would never be hers. He looked at it again, folded the cloth back in place, and tucked the small bundle back into his bag. He shook his head and looked again at the buckskin horse, stand-ing in its stall and munching oats. That brought a smile to him. Life wasn't bad, even if it got mourn-ful at times.

Monte rolled over and reached for his boots. It was time to throw some water on his face and find a cooked meal. If a fellow was going to spend some time in town, he might as well make it worth his while.

Back on the street again, he saw no hint of any-one he knew. Everything looked calm, and he thought he had done right by leaving his gun in the stable. He looked up and down the main street until he saw a sign for a café. Crossing the street and stepping up onto the sidewalk, he made his way there in a couple of minutes.

The café was empty except for a dark-featured woman in back, who was not very visible because the light was not strong inside. Daylight from the evening sun slanted in through the west-facing win-dows, and no one had lit any lamps yet. Monte saw half a dozen square tables, three to each side as he faced the kitchen. He stood by the second table on his right, letting his eyes adjust to the dim interior.

The woman came forward, and he could see her better now. She had long, dark hair that hung loosely behind her shoulders. She had a dark complexion and looked as if she might be Mexican, although this far north it was more likely she was Indian. She was wearing a white apron and a loose, dark-striped cotton dress, but she looked as if she had a nice figure. She was older than a girl, but she was still young and pretty, he decided.

Her dark eyes met Monte's as she smiled and said, "Would you like to sit down?"

"Thanks," he said, taking off his coat and sitting at the table to his right. He looked up at the young woman and felt himself smiling. He took off his hat.

"Would you like to order something?"

Monte realized he had smelled food since he walked in, but he had been intent on getting his vision and bearings up until this moment. "Yes," he answered. "I'd like something to eat."

"Well," she went on, bringing her two hands together in front of the white apron, "we have the regular things. Bacon, ham, beefsteaks, potatoes, onions." She shook her head. "No chicken or eggs right now." Then she smiled again. "And I do have a nice stew. Everyone likes that."

Monte thought it might have been the stew that he smelled. It had a good aroma, not like some stews that had sat too long in otherwise reputable kitchens. He had come into this place with the general notion of eating steak and potatoes, but his impressions of the moment changed that. "I'll try the stew," he said.

"Good," she answered. "I think you'll like it." She

turned and walked away, toward the back of the café.

Monte watched her as she walked. For a working girl she had a graceful way about her. She had made him feel comfortable from the first moment. He had decided by now, mainly from the tone of her voice, that she was Mexican. He had been among Mexicans enough in the Southwest that he could hear even the faintest accent from those who had spoken English all their lives. She really had a pretty voice, he thought.

He smiled. He had probably liked her before he heard her speak, and she had probably sensed it. He had noticed it down south. Her people could tell at first glance if a person wanted to be friends. They could probably tell the ones who didn't, too. Monte had always gotten good treatment, and he had imagined some of it came in response to the way he presented himself.

Not all cowpunchers were that way, especially the ones he had met in the South who had kept their old ways. They despised Mexicans, Negroes, Indians—anything that didn't look like them and think like them. The southerners who came north and stayed on had a tendency, most of them, to fit in with the new country. But even at that, they would still call a Mexican a greaser, using the language they grew up with. If they had never accepted a Mexican as a full human being, they wouldn't have known to think or speak differently. Monte imagined that lots of the cowpunchers and freighters who stopped in here would see things in that same way, seeing a Mexican when this woman came to the table. And that would set the tone of their exchange.

He watched the young woman as she came back to his table with a large bowl. As she set it down he could see pieces of meat, potatoes, carrots, and onions.

"Looks good."

"I hope you like it," she said, reaching down to set a spoon on the table next to his right hand.

"Thanks."

"Would you like some coffee?"

"Not right now, thanks. Probably later."

"All right." She walked away and left him to eat his meal.

Monte dug in with the spoon, and he liked the stew well enough. He liked the combination of tastes, and the meat wasn't tough and chewy. He guessed she had made the stew for midday dinner and it had simmered well.

When he finished the first bowl of stew she brought him a second, which he also ate alone as she rattled a few things in the kitchen. She came out again as he finished his second serving.

"Would you like some coffee now?"

"Sure," he said. "That sounds good."

"And cake?"

Monte felt himself frown. He hadn't cared too much for Mexican cakes and sweet breads. "Have you got any pie?"

She pursed her mouth as she shook her head. "No, not today. I'll bake pies tomorrow."

Monte raised his eyebrows. "Well, I guess I could try the cake."

She smiled and nodded. "All right. I'll bring it."

In a couple of minutes she was back with a tan mug of dark, steaming coffee, accompanied by a small white plate with a square of yellow cake on it. She set the coffee and dessert on the table, and from a pocket of her apron she took out a fork. Monte hadn't seen where the spoon had come from before, and he found himself smiling at his simple new knowledge.

As he looked up at her he thought he might like to share a few words before someone else walked in.

"My name's Monte," he said. "Monte Casteel." Feeling gallant, he added, "You can add my name to the list of admirers who like your stew."

"Thank you," she answered, with her face relaxed and her eyes shining. "My name is Ramona. Some people call me Mrs. Flynn."

Monte felt his spirits sink, but he goaded himself back up. If this was just a moment of friendship, it shouldn't matter if she was married. "Well, I'm pleased to meet you," he said. "You have a very nice café here."

"Thank you." She paused, then motioned with her head and drew her eyebrows together. "Go ahead. You can eat while we talk."

Monte took a sip of his coffee and then cut into his cake. He looked up.

"Are you staying over, or are you passing through?" she asked.

"I'm staying over at least tonight," he said. Then he ate the bite of cake and took another sip of his coffee.

"That's good."

"Uh-huh. I'll get plenty of other chances to sleep out in the cold." He took another bite of cake, and he noticed it had more flavor than he had expected. Then he realized he had made a mistake in assuming what kind of cake it would be.

"Are you going to a ranch?"

Monte took a drink of coffee and appreciated the question. He knew she could tell he was a cowpuncher from the cut of his clothes, so she was asking where, if anyplace, he worked.

"I'm in between jobs right now," he said, looking up at her. "Most of the fall work is over."

"That's good."

Monte spoke without thinking. "Why?" As he asked the question, he realized her phrase might have been just an automatic one to keep the conversation going, or it might have meant something to her that he did not see. He felt a flicker of guilt for his quick response.

Her words were soft. "Oh, well—I mean, it must be good to be done with work for a while, so you can rest."

"Oh, uh-huh," he said, feeling a little better.

She spoke again. "I hope you enjoy your stay here."

He was afraid she was closing the conversation, so he asked, "What kind of pie do you plan to fix tomorrow?"

"I have to use dried fruit, you know. Last week I made apple pie, so this week I'll make it with apricots."

Her face was bright, and he could feel his spirits

lifting again. "You know how to cook all this good food, don't you?"

She wiped her hands on her apron. "Oh, sure."

He paused with his coffee cup halfway to his mouth. "Even speckled puppy?"

She laughed. "Raisins and rice? Oh, sure. I cook it in a pot."

"How'd you learn to cook these things?"

Her face lost a little of its shine. "From my husband, Mr. Flynn. He knew how to cook all these things. He said he learned to cook spotted puppy in a flour sack."

Monte looked toward the back of the café. "Is he not around anymore?"

"No," she said. "He died last year."

"I'm sorry to hear that."

"It's all right. We try to keep going, you know, and we try not to get too sad about something that already happened and we can't change."

Monte nodded and ate more cake.

"It's God's will," she said.

"Uh-huh." He drank from his coffee.

"But anyway," she said, drawing a breath, "we try to keep going, and we try to see the good things and be happy."

Monte looked at her as he set his cup down. "We?"

"My people, you know. It's the way I was raised. So even if I'm here by myself, I remember it all."

"That's good," he said, realizing he was speaking her language.

"Uh-huh," she said, speaking his.

He felt the cloud had lifted again. "Well, if I'm

still around here tomorrow, I'll make a point of trying out your homemade apricot pie."

She smiled as she said, "That would be nice."

He finished the cake and complimented it, and she took away the plate and fork. She came back with a coffeepot, and as she was refilling his cup, another person came into the café.

Monte turned and saw a young cowpuncher, probably in his early twenties, wearing woolly chaps, a canvas jacket, and a tipped-back hat. The hat had a slightly curled brim and a round crown, and in its position it gave the young man a jaunty, carefree look. He had dark brown hair falling down on his forehead, and his mustache turned up with his smile.

"Hi, Johnny," came Ramona's voice.

"Hi there, Ramona." The young cowboy nodded at Monte and moved to the opposite table, where he stood with his back to the kitchen as he took off his coat.

Monte, noticing the gun and holster hanging outside the woolly chaps, realized the young man was seating himself so that he wouldn't have his back to the door. Monte raised his eyebrows. Without having given it much thought, he had sat so he could keep an eye on the waitress.

The puncher sat back from the table with his spurred right boot resting on his left knee. "Just coffee," he said, looking up and smiling, as Ramona appeared at his side.

Monte noticed that beneath the red bandanna a horsehair watch chain led down and looped into the young man's left vest pocket. He seemed like a happy young puncher, the type who would spend long winter hours braiding horsehair into a watch chain or hatband.

Ramona came with another tan mug and the coffeepot, and as she was pouring the coffee with her back turned toward Monte, she said something in a low voice. The young man said something back.

Monte heard the boot touch the floor and the chair scoot forward as Ramona came toward him with the coffeepot. He glanced at his cup, which was still full, and she glanced at it too.

"This boy over here works for a ranch that's looking for help," she said in her soft voice. "I don't know if you're looking for work, but he's a nice boy."

"Thanks," he said with a half-smile.

"I'm going to go light some lamps," she said as she moved away.

Monte looked across at the puncher named Johnny, who looked back and smiled.

"Come on over, stranger," the young man called out as he motioned with his left hand. "Come on over and have a cup of coffee with me."

Monte nodded and said, "I think I will." He picked up his hat, coat, and coffee cup and moved across to Johnny's table.

The young man rose from his chair and held out his hand. "Name's Johnny Romaine," he said. "And pleased to meet you."

Monte set down his coffee cup and shook hands. "Mine's Monte Casteel. Pleased to meet you, too."

"Have a seat."

"Thanks." Monte set his hat and coat on the next chair and sat down.

"Some weather, uh?"

Monte reflected. "Oh, the wind was a little stiff for a while there." Then, feeling that he was invited to say more, he added, "I was ridin' straight into it for a good part of the day." That was as good as saying he had ridden north.

"Oh, uh-huh." Johnny sipped at his coffee. "Movin' on, are you?"

"Not in any hurry."

"Uh-huh. Well, this is good country to see."

"I'd agree, from what I've seen." Monte paused and then asked, "Do you winter here?"

"That I do," said Johnny. "I ride for the Three-Bar Durham Ranch. The Old Man kept me on last winter, and he asked me to stay on again."

"That sounds good enough."

"I'd say. Winter wages come in handy."

Monte felt it was his opening again. "I just finished up the fall season down on the MT, out of Cheyenne."

"Is that right." Johnny said it more as a statement than a question. Then he asked, "Good outfit?"

Monte raised his eyebrows and turned down his mouth. "Good enough."

Johnny took another drink of coffee and said, "This one's all right. The Old Man treats us fair. Good eats, too."

"Uh-huh. What's the Old Man's name?" Monte was pretty sure it wouldn't be Elswick, and he hoped it wasn't Lurie.

"Thane. Andrew Thane." Johnny sniffed. "He told

me that if I ran into a likely fella that was lookin' for work for a month or two, he could use a hand."

Monte hesitated, but he liked the young puncher's approach. "Well, I wasn't really lookin' for work, but I can always use the wages. It's a long time till spring."

"Isn't that right." Johnny toyed with his coffee cup and looked across the table at Monte. "Well, if you're interested, you could ride on out with me and talk to the Old Man. It's his say, of course."

"How far out is it? I'm already put up for the night."

"It's about ten miles southwest of here. But if you want to talk to the Old Man, you might want to ride out first thing in the morning. I think he's goin' to be gone in the afternoon."

"Uh-huh." Monte twisted his mouth. That meant he might miss the apricot pie, but if he ended up staying around for a while, he would probably have a chance to drop by here again. "I think I might do that," he said.

"That sounds fine. I'll tell the Old Man this evening. I think he'll like it."

Monte had a second thought. "Is there anything he might expect me to do, other than the regular chores?"

"Just stay out of trouble."

Monte had a fleeting impression of three men on the trail. "I think I've had some practice at that," he said.

Chapter Three

On the way out to the Three-Bar Ranch the next morning, Monte had time to think things over. As he had told Johnny Romaine, he was in no hurry to move on. Now, as he turned it over in his mind, he took a look at his own motives.

He didn't want to be staying on just because he knew Dora lived in the vicinity. There had been a time when he would walk down a street because he had walked it with her, or he would walk up a set of stairs and touch the railing that she had touched. He knew that if there were any of that left in him, he needed to get it out.

He also didn't want to be staying around just because Elswick had told him not to. He believed what he had said to Romaine, that he practiced staying out of trouble. On the other hand, he couldn't let a high-handed bully run him off if he felt like staying.

If he wasn't staying because of Dora or because of Elswick, he had to admit to himself that each of them contributed some influence. He wasn't sure, but maybe he did have an inner sense that staying awhile would help him get her out of his blood, and maybe he did have a sense that if he didn't let Elswick tell him what to do, he could settle things with himself on his own terms.

Then there was a matter of a couple of months' wages. If they were honest wages, they were nothing to sniff at. A rider like himself was welcome to ride the grub line, as it was called. He could stop at one ranch or another for a few days, doing odd jobs in exchange for board and room, but he didn't look forward to a whole winter of that. Winter wages could make a difference.

And, of course, there was Ramona. If he had been in no hurry before he met her, he was in less of a hurry afterward. He had liked her from the first minute, and he thought there might have been a spark of interest on her side, too. A job at the Three-Bar would give him a chance to see more of her.

Out here in the open country, away from the complications, it did seem as if a fellow could think more clearly. He knew that as he sat in the café that evening, he had wanted to stay over an extra day just so he could see her again. Now, as he imagined lolling around the livery stable or loafing around town for a day or maybe more, he saw that he could have slipped back into the same sort of powerlessness, if not mooning and moping, that he was trying to get out of.

He remembered what she looked like standing by the table, and he felt a broad smile come to his face. He sure did hope to see her again. He wondered if she had any callers. She didn't seem all that sweet on the kid Johnny Romaine, but there were plenty of other fellows out on the scattered ranches. Well, the only way to know was to find out. If he liked the looks of things at the Three-Bar, that could help him stay around and learn more about her.

As his thoughts turned again to the trail ahead, he wondered what kind of man Thane would be. Johnny had called him "the Old Man," but that just meant he was the boss of his own outfit. Romaine was pretty young, too. He had gone on to tell Monte he had worked a couple of years in Ten Sleep before working at the Three-Bar, but still he wasn't very old. Thane must have some confidence in him, though, to rely on the young man's recommendations. Of course, as Johnny had said, it would be up to the Old Man.

Monte rode into the Three-Bar at midmorning. He approached it from the open side on the east. The ranch buildings lay in a sheltered cove with hills to the north and west, while on the south side a creek flowed eastward. All along the creek the trees were leafless, mostly cottonwoods and box elders and willows, but up in the crevices and draws behind the buildings he saw dark cedar trees alone and in small bunches.

The building in the middle was a ranch house. It

was a square structure with wood shingles, a bat-and-board exterior, and a stone chimney on the north side. The house faced east, with a porch that would catch sun on cool mornings and give shade on hot afternoons. To the left of the house and closer to Monte, facing north and with corrals in back, stood a long barn with no hayloft. Across from the barn some fifty or sixty yards was the bunkhouse, which also faced inward. The bunkhouse had two doors and looked as if it had been built and then added on to. Both sections had horizontal boards for the outer walls, and the nearer section had a porch. Smoke was curling out of a stovepipe in the second section, so Monte supposed that part was the cookhouse.

The ground between the buildings was hard-packed and bare, with pocks and ruts but no fences or trees or flower beds. From droppings on the ground it was evident that cattle had roamed through the yard. Monte could see where they had clipped the weeds along the edges of the buildings. As he rode farther into the yard, he saw a woodpile and a lumber pile at the far end of the bunkhouse. Somewhere there was probably a trash pile for cans and bottles and other rubbish, but what he could see was neat and clean.

A man appeared at the cookhouse doorway. "Boss is in here," he called out.

Monte raised his hand in acknowledgment and then turned his horse in toward the hitching rail in front of the porch. Leaving the buckskin at the rail, he walked to the cookhouse door, taking off his gloves as he went.

The same man was at the doorway again. Monte got a better look at him now. He was of average height and build, with dark hair thinning on top and running to gray on the sides.

"Come on in," he said.

Monte took off his hat and stepped into the eating area, where a man with reddish hair and beard was rising from the mess table.

"How do you do?" he said, holding out his hand. "I'm Andrew Thane."

As Monte shook hands he said, "Just fine. I'm Monte Casteel. Pleased to meet you."

"So am I. Well, come on in and sit down. Johnny told me I might expect you. Oh, by the way, this is the cook, Horace."

Monte and Horace shook hands and exchanged civilities, and then Monte sat down at the same side of the table as Thane. He saw now that the Old Man was about forty years old, with his thick waves of strawberry hair going silver, as was his beard. He had good teeth and hazel eyes, and his ruddy complexion helped give him a jovial aspect. He was not heavy, though. His gray vest, with the golden watch chain lying against it, did not strain at the buttons.

Thane picked up a curved-stem pipe from a flattened-down can on the table, and he drew a cloud of smoke out of it. "Horace is making some more coffee," he said. "Feel free to smoke if you like."

"That's all right. I don't usually."

Thane smiled, and Monte could see the teeth clenched on the pipe stem.

Horace set down a white crockery cup in front of

Monte and went back to the kitchen. Monte saw that the other two cups on the table had already been used.

Taking the pipe from his mouth, the Old Man said, "Johnny tells me you look like a good hand."

"I try to be."

"You look like it to me, too."

"Thank you, sir."

The boss moved his pipe toward his mouth and then paused. "What I'm looking for is a general, all-around hand for a couple of months."

Monte nodded.

"Not a bronc twister, or a fella who just ropes, or any other specialty, you know."

"Uh-huh."

"I pay thirty a month, plus room and board, of course."

Monte frowned. He had been making forty.

"That's winter wages," added the boss. "Days are shorter, and you have more time to eat." He smiled. "In the summer I pay forty."

Monte thought for a second. "That sounds all right, I guess."

"Well, that's just fine. I'm glad to have another hand, and I'm sure Horace is, too."

Monte looked up and saw Horace with a blackened coffeepot. Horace's smile confirmed that there was wood to be chopped and meat to be butchered.

Thane held up his left hand. "No more coffee for me, thanks. I think I need to be on my way." He pulled out his gold watch, opened the case, and closed it. "If I leave for Lurie's now, I'll have time to get there and back before dark."

Horace finished pouring Monte's coffee and then asked, "Is Johnny going with you?"

"I don't see a need for it right now." Thane puffed on his pipe.

Horace filled his own cup and took the coffeepot away.

Thane rose from his seat and picked up a gray wool overcoat from the chair next to him. Then he went to the doorway, where he lifted a hat from a nail on the wall. It was a light-colored hat with a high crown pinched on all four sides, and it sat well when he fitted it onto his head. As he opened the door he turned to look at Monte. "Make yourself at home, young man. If you need something to do, ask Horace or Johnny." He paused to rap his pipe on the outside of the doorjamb, and then he closed the door behind him.

Horace came back and sat down to drink coffee, and the two of them made small talk for a while. Monte learned that Horace used to work for an outfit called the Muleshoe down in Colorado, and he was particular to say that it had nothing to do with the town in Texas by the same name. He spoke like a man who had had a little education, but he also used language as loose as any that Monte had heard around the corrals. Eventually he got around to telling Monte that there was no hurry to do anything until after dinner.

"Go ahead and pick out a bunk and get settled in," he said. "Johnny'll be in for dinner. After that I can send you out to hunt firewood. I like cedar the best, and when we're not pressed, it's worth a little extra time to find it. You'll have to ride out a little

45

further, because most of it anywhere near the ranch has been picked pretty clean—anything down and dead, anyway. You sure don't want to cut anything green."

Monte went ahead and unpacked his gear, then took his horse to the barn, unsaddled him, and turned him into the corral. He assumed he would ride Three-Bar horses, and the buckskin could rest up and eat company grass and hay.

Johnny Romaine came into the bunkhouse at about noontime and hung his hat on a peg above his bunk. Monte noticed he wasn't wearing the horsehair watch chain, so he assumed it was something Johnny wore when he went to town. Otherwise, the young man was dressed just as he had been the day before, including the woolly chaps and six-gun.

"Looks like the Old Man put you on, then."

"He sure did."

"Well, good. Like I said before, this is a good place to work, and the grub's fine, too."

Horace served up dinner from a pot of beef and beans, with a couple of tin plates of biscuits. All three men ate without much hurry but with very little talk. Horace poured coffee afterward and then tended to the dishes.

Johnny Romaine rolled himself a neat cigarette and lit it. "So the Old Man went to see Lurie?"

"That's what he said."

"Lurie's got his place to the north of us," Johnny said, motioning with his head in that general direction.

"I've heard of him," Monte offered.

"Good or bad?"

"Neither. Just that he had a ranch up this way."

"Well, that he does. Him and the Old Man get along all right, and I think they're puttin' their heads together."

"Oh, is that right?"

"Yeah, it seems like this other fellow over to the east, by the name of Elswick, wants to try to push everyone else out."

"That doesn't surprise me."

Johnny held the cigarette an inch away from his mouth. "Oh, do you know him?"

"I met him on the trail out south of town yesterday. He told me I was on his land and ought to keep movin'."

Johnny sniffed. "He's got a lot of nerve. He just doesn't want any lone riders hangin' around and gettin' put on at one of these other outfits. Hell, that land isn't his. It isn't anybody's."

"That's what I thought. I figured he had about the same kind of claims as anyone else."

"He might have a little more. He came in here about four years ago, they say, and he's had several different riders take out claims for him. Naturally, he'll get that land transferred into his name after they get clear title to it."

"Oh, yeah."

Johnny took another drag and exhaled. "And for the last couple of years, he's been bringin' in hardcases now and then."

"I think I met one of them yesterday, too."

"Ol' Snake Eyes?"

"That sounds like him. Goes by the name of Pool."

"Uh-huh. That's him. Did you notice his spurs? They've got rowels like a Mexican's. They look like they were filed out of silver dollars. Some fellas do that."

Monte nodded. Most rowels, including his own, were the size of a two-bit piece. "I saw it down south quite a bit."

Johnny spit a fleck of tobacco. "He's a bad one. I bet he has to take 'em off to sneak up on someone. He probably has a black slicker for night work, too." Then, as if conscious that he had said a little too much, he sat back and looked at the end of his cigarette as he took another pull.

Monte sipped at his coffee. "So you think Thane and Lurie expect Elswick to make a move?"

"Hard to say what he might do, but that seems to be what they're thinkin'."

"Uh-huh."

"Yeah. When roundup was over, Lurie and the Old Man paid off all their seasonal men, and things emptied out. About that time the sheriff had to go to Denver to get his insides purged—he's got parasites—and the next thing we know, Elswick brings in old Snake Eyes. It doesn't look good."

"So Thane and Lurie are both hiring men?"

"For a little balance, I think. The Old Man just wanted to put on another hand, and that's all Lurie has done. Just someone extra to help keep an eye on things."

"Oh, did Lurie hire someone new?"

"Yeah. Fellow named Weaver." Johnny yawned

and then said, "The Old Man doesn't want any trouble. But he knows he needs to show he's ready if he needs to be."

"That sounds like it," Monte said. "He seemed to me—Elswick, that is—that he wanted to run the whole country."

"That's it in a nutshell." Johnny stubbed out his cigarette in the can with flattened sides. "And it's not like it's the first time."

"Oh?"

Johnny took a drink of coffee. "Well, you'll hear it sooner or later. They say he used to have his own outfit over on the Badwater, way west of here. He got into some trouble there, and a sheepherder got killed."

"Huh. When I told him I was going west, he told me it was better country there. I wondered why he'd say that—and if he thought it, why he was over here."

Horace set down his cup of coffee and took a chair. "There's a little more to the story than Johnny told you so far."

Monte looked at Johnny, who looked at Horace and said, "Go ahead."

Horace leveled his gaze at Monte and said, "The story is, he got into a jackpot with another man's wife. Got her het up to leave him, I guess, and left her holdin' the bag."

Monte raised his eyebrows. "Just backed out?"

Horace shrugged. "The other fellow might have sent him a word or two. I don't know. And then there was the sheepherder business, which in itself wouldn't have run him off but could have helped."

Horace took a sip of coffee and set his cup down. "Anyway, that's the story we heard. He sold out and left."

Monte gave a low whistle. "So he just came over here and got started up again, huh?"

Horace nodded. "He's got no shame. Hell, you know how word travels. And he acts like he's got all the right in the world."

"You wonder where he comes from," Monte said.

"From somewhere around Illinois, I think. If he ever had any principles, he sloughed 'em off little by little on his way out. Some fellas start out mean or rough and just take their bad manners with 'em, but this fella seems to have done it the other way." Horace looked at Johnny. "Doesn't that seem about right?"

Johnny nodded. "I guess. I know I don't trust him. Not him or his hired gun, Snake Eyes."

"Now, he's a mean one," Horace said. "I bet he's always been that way."

Monte spoke up. "Where do you think he's from?"

Johnny answered. "You usually think that type comes from Texas, but I've heard him talk, and I think he might be from Missouri."

"I didn't hear him say anything."

"He's got a funny voice," Johnny said. "But I don't think he's from Texas."

"You know he's from somewhere down there," Horace said, "just from the looks of him. But they're not all like that from down there. Hell, we had some good Texans at the Muleshoe, and we've had some good ones here. But a lot of these gunmen do come from down there, and they're that way by nature. They grow up thinkin' a gun is a superior way to solve an argument. They say fist-fightin' is 'nigger stuff,' and they think every Mexican you meet has got a foot-long pigsticker."

Monte thought for a moment and then said, "So they're specialists."

"That's what they are," Horace said. "They want to fight, and they've got one way to do it. This fellow Pool, I'd say he was that way where he came from, and if he makes it back he'll be the same."

The conversation cooled down after that, and a little while later the two punchers went out to the barn. Johnny showed Monte the horse he could ride that afternoon, and the two of them roped out their mounts. Johnny said he was going to ride to the south to check on things, and he added that Monte would probably have the best luck if he rode west. The two men brushed their horses and saddled them without saying much, and then they walked the horses out into the ranch yard.

"You shouldn't have any trouble out that way," Johnny added. "It's only when we go east, over El-swick's way, that we ride two together. I don't have any worries about goin' south on my own, and the Old Man didn't worry about goin' north to Lurie's by himself."

The two riders mounted up, waved goodbye, and went their separate ways.

In all that afternoon, Monte did not see another rider. Several times he saw red Durham cattle with the Three-Bar brand. They looked as if they were going into winter in good shape, as did the Herefords and mixed breeds he saw here and there.

51

He did find three small, dead cedar trees, which he dragged to a common spot and then roped together for the drag back to the ranch. He had noticed that the woodpile wasn't dangerously low, so he imagined he had done all right for the afternoon's work. In addition to finding the three trees, he was able to see quite a bit of country to the west.

As he thought over the conversation they had had after dinner, he decided Johnny was an easy talker if he trusted someone. Horace, of course, was a man of some worldly knowledge and was willing to share it.

After supper, when he and Johnny were stretched out on their bunks, Monte led into a topic he was interested in knowing more about. He spoke without looking directly at Johnny.

"That lady Ramona who runs the café sure is nice, isn't she?"

"Oh, yeah," Johnny said back.

"Do you know much about her?"

"No, not much. Just that she's a widow and a good cook."

"She told me she was a widow. How did her husband die?"

"Who, Flynn? Oh, he got caught in a blizzard about a year and a half ago. It was too bad."

"Sounds like it." Monte paused, and still not looking at Johnny, he said, "I think she's kinda pretty."

"Yeah, I guess so. I hadn't really looked at her that way."

That's good, Monte thought. Then he said out loud, "Does she have a beau?"

"Nah, not that I know of." Johnny sat up, smiling. "Are you sweet on her?"

Monte looked over and grinned. "Oh, I don't know. But I'd sure like to see her again."

Chapter Four

Monte woke up in the dark of morning. The air inside the bunkhouse felt chilly on his face, and he knew it was time to get up. Hearing faint sounds from the cookhouse, he knew Horace was working up breakfast. He wanted to be up and at it before Horace came to the door and growled, so he rolled out of his bunk.

He had heard Thane come in when he and Johnny had retired to the bunkhouse the evening before, and he wondered if there would be anything come out of the boss's visit to Lurie. Monte sensed that trouble was in the making, even if everyone was smiling and had nothing more serious for him to do than to go out and hunt firewood. Johnny and Horace were both easygoing, he thought, but they must be wound up a little tight, judging from the way the talk flowed out about Elswick and Pool. It would be interesting to see if Thane had anything new.

As Monte's eyes adjusted to the room, he saw that Johnny Romaine was already up and gone. Monte made quick work of getting dressed, splashing water on his face, and smoothing out his mustache, all without taking the trouble of lighting a lamp. When he walked into the warm cookhouse, the room seemed bright, although Horace had only one lamp burning. Monte smelled bacon and coffee, which made everything seem in order. Johnny, seated at the table drinking coffee, looked up to say good morning.

Monte poured himself a cup of coffee and sat down across from Johnny. In another minute, Horace brought a plate of crisp bacon and a plate of fried potatoes from the kitchen. Johnny looked across at Monte as if to say, "See, didn't I tell you it was good eats?" Then the two of them went to work on breakfast.

The door opened, and Monte saw the white crown of Thane's hat. The boss was looking down as he was scraping the sole of his boot, and he must have wanted a little light to finish the task. He stepped into the room, closed the door, and hung his hat on the nail.

"Good mornin', boys."

"Good mornin'," they said together.

Without taking off his gray overcoat, Thane sat down next to Monte and served himself coffee. "A little chilly out there," he said as he put a spoonful of sugar into his cup.

His two men mumbled, "Uh-huh."

Thane served himself bacon and potatoes and began eating.

The meal went on with hardly any talk. Horace brought two more plates of grub and sat down across from Thane to have his meal. Johnny finished first, and after taking his plate and fork to the dishpan, he sat down again at the table and poured himself more coffee. Monte finished his meal and did the same.

Johnny pushed himself back from the table as if he were going to roll a cigarette, but he didn't. He just cocked his right boot up onto his left knee and put his right hand into his vest pocket.

Monte imagined the young cowpuncher wanted to have a smoke but was waiting for the Old Man to finish eating. Then he saw Johnny's hand move inside the vest pocket, in what he took to be fidgeting. He heard a little clicking sound, like someone rubbing a pair of dice together. The movement stopped, and then it started again.

Monte looked across at Johnny and gave him a questioning look.

Johnny gave him a look of mild surprise and then apparently registered the question. "Oh," he said. "These." He drew his hand out of his pocket and held it, palm up, over his edge of the table. "Elk's teeth."

Monte straightened up and saw the two yellowish teeth, each with a round, knobby end tapering into a shank. "Oh, uh-huh." He knew some fellows carried them for good luck.

Johnny put the ivories back into his pocket. "Just somethin' to carry around," he said.

Thane turned to Monte and winked. "Johnny wants to find a girl to give 'em to."

Monte looked across the table, and Johnny smiled. "I can't deny that. That's what happened to the last pair. But there's more where these came from."

Everyone laughed, and in a couple of more minutes Thane finished eating. He took his plate and fork to the dishpan and came back to his chair, taking his pipe out of his coat pocket as he sat down. He brought out a leather pouch of tobacco, and as he began stuffing his pipe, Johnny brought out his bag of makin's. Horace was still eating, so Monte inferred that Johnny had been waiting for the Old Man to bring out his pipe.

In a little while the air in the room became hazy, as the tobacco smoke mixed with the smell of coffee and bacon and kerosene fumes. Monte thought it would be just as well to get out into the cold, clear morning. He sat and waited. Johnny smoked his cigarette down close and snuffed it in the flattened can. Then the Old Man took his pipe from his mouth and spoke.

"Johnny, you can ride west this morning and take a look at things." He turned in his chair. "And Monte, you can carry on with what you were doin' yesterday. Of course, you can keep your eyes open, too."

Both punchers acknowledged the orders and stood up when the Old Man was finished speaking. They put on their hats and coats and stepped outside.

"It *is* cold," Johnny said as they put on their gloves.

The air was dry and sharp as Monte drew it in through his nose. "It sure is," he said.

When they had roped out and saddled their horses for the morning's work, Johnny said, "I wouldn't mind walkin' 'em out for a ways."

"All right," Monte said. He had had more than one horse buck on a cold morning, and since he didn't know these horses yet and Johnny did, it sounded like a good idea.

It was a still morning, with clear sounds—the clip-clop of horse hooves, the squeak of saddle leather, the faint jingle of spurs—as the men led the horses out of the barn. They had warmed the bits under their coats before putting the bridles on, but Johnny's horse was still biting at his and making clunking sounds.

"Sort of a biter, uh?" Monte asked.

"Oh, he's always that way." Johnny smiled.

A hundred yards out from the barn, the men checked their cinches. "You get on first," Johnny said.

Monte put his foot in the stirrup and swung on, wondering if the horse was going to go into a fit, but everything stayed calm. Then Johnny swung on, and as soon as his right leg came down, the dark horse started bucking. The woolly chaps went up and down but didn't flop; Monte could see Johnny was hooked in good with his spurs. After half a dozen bucks the horse leveled out and ran, giving a crow hop every twenty yards or so. Johnny rode the horse out and turned it around, then came trotting back.

"I think he's ready now," he said, grinning. "We can ride out together a ways if you want."

Monte agreed, and the two of them turned west and rode out around the north side of the ranch buildings.

When the bunkhouse was down on their left, Johnny said, "I bet Horace and the Old Man are schemin' at this very minute."

"What on?"

"Well, Horace is tryin' to convince him he needs an icehouse."

"Really?"

"Uh-huh. Now, the Old Man, he wants to find himself a wife. I think you can tell that. And Horace, he wants an icehouse. I think he's told the Old Man it would be a nice thing for the missus."

Monte looked down at his horse's gait and then looked back up at Johnny. "Well, I guess it would."

Johnny gave a quick nod. "I suppose so too. But someone would either have to cut ice or make ice every day, all winter. Horace might make the ice, but I think he'd have someone else go out and cut it." He gave Monte a knowing look.

"I see. And I suppose someone would have to build the thing, too."

"That's right."

Monte thought for a second. "What kind does he want to build?"

"I don't know. I think maybe somethin' like a dugout or a root cellar, but I haven't asked for details."

"Maybe he just wants to keep us busy."

"Oh, yeah. If it's not one thing, it's another. If we were drawin' gunfighter wages we'd be sittin' around with our feet up on the stove, but we're not, and that's fine. I'd just as soon be doin' somethin'."

"Me too."

Monte hunted firewood all morning. As on the day before, he saw cattle off and on, with nothing to cause concern. Twice along creeks he found plenty of the softer firewood, and in one of the places he saw a good stand of cottonwoods that would be useful for the roof of a dugout or a root cellar. He made mental note of those places and went on to look for cedar. There really wasn't a lot of dead cedar; the trees he found in this rolling country were short, slow-growing things. He knew that up on the mountain there would be larger ones, fit for logs and fence posts. Down here, most of them were not much taller than a man on horseback. Nearly all of them were green, going into their russet winter color, and doing well.

He found two dead trees in the course of the morning—small trees, like the ones he had found the day before. As he dragged them back to the ranch he thought it really wasn't very productive work, but it didn't cost Horace anything. He wondered if Thane had other work in mind for him, such as building an icehouse, or if he would keep on coming up with busywork as he waited to see what Elswick would do.

At dinnertime, Monte mentioned the places where he had seen good deadfall and timber. Thane took interest and said it would be a good idea to bring in a wagonload or two before the next snow-fall came. So that afternoon, the two hired men brought in a load of firewood. Some of it was already broken into stove lengths, but most of it would need to be cut at least once.

It seemed as if Thane could work an idea down into parts. The next morning, he showed Johnny a drawing he had made of a fireplace poker, with a pointed end and a back hook. He told his young right-hand man to fire up the forge and see what he could do. Horace showed Monte where the ax was and then put him to work on the woodpile. As Monte took the ax and went at his work, he recalled Johnny Romaine's comment that if it wasn't one thing it was another. Or, as he had heard many times, it all paid the same. It was winter wages, whether he was working on fire or working on ice.

Monte started in on the cedar trees, having decided they would be the hardest. It took quite a bit of work to hack or knock off the smaller branches, and then the trunks were hard and bouncy. It was slow work, but it warmed him up. Before long he had taken off his coat and gloves. He liked the free movement and better grip as his muscles loosened and the ax hit just where he wanted it to. It was a pleasure to do a thing well.

After he had been at it for about an hour, he decided to take a breather. As he had been cutting the larger pieces he had caught a whiff now and then of the cedar fragrance. Now at his leisure, he picked up a wood chip and smelled it. It smelled like cedar, but not very strong. He got up from his rest and laid a stove length upright next to the chopping block. Then he took the ax, split the piece of wood, and smelled the freshly exposed inside. It had the rich aroma, dry and sharp, of real cedar. He could understand why women liked it for the chests and dressers where they put their most delicate clothing. The milled lumber would have more surface. On a hunch he went into the bunkhouse where he had found the ax, and he lifted the bucksaw from its nail. Back outside, he found a piece he would have to cut anyway, and he sawed it crosswise. The fragrance came up nicely as he sawed; the two smooth, pink cross-sections had a fine smell, also. The ax was faster, though, so he went back to work with it.

In the latter part of the morning he heard horses. Laying the ax against the woodpile, he walked out into the yard. Two men, strangers to Monte, were riding in. Monte saw movement at his left, and he turned to see Horace at the cookhouse door.

"Boss is in the house," he called out.

The man closest to the bunkhouse raised his hand and nodded. He was a clean-shaven man with his face fleshing out. He wore a brown hat and a thick wool overcoat, also brown. His gray wool trousers were tucked into dark brown stovepipe boots. He was probably in his mid-thirties; he looked as if he was in that stage of life when some men put on weight. He had the air about him of a man who would like to be governor waving his gloved hand at the voters. Monte guessed it was Carson Lurie.

The other man, who had the appearance of a hired hand, wore a denim work coat and denim pants, with no chaps. He wore a light brown hat with a narrow brim, low crown, and two wide creases with a center ridge. Monte could not see his face very well, but it was fair-skinned and framed with light brown hair.

The two men rode past Monte, giving him a short wave. Monte waved back.

The men rode up to the house and dismounted. The man in brown handed his reins to the man in denims, who turned and walked toward the barn with the two horses following. Ringing sounds were coming out of the east end of the barn, and it looked as if the cowpuncher was going to go visit with someone he knew as his equal.

Monte went back to chopping wood. He looked at the sun and figured he had about an hour to go until dinner. The visitors would probably stay for dinner, and he could wait until then to find out who they were.

Monte had chopped up all five cedar trees and had gone to work on the easier stuff when Horace beat the triangle at the cookhouse door. Monte didn't need a second call. He laid the ax against the woodpile, picked up his gloves and coat, and went in to clean up. As he was drying off, Johnny Romaine came in with the other rider, whom he introduced as Farrell.

Monte got a better look at him now. He had freckles, washed-out blue eyes, and a hard look on his face. He wore a shirt with two breast pockets and buttons all the way down the front, a rather expensive shirt that did away with the need for a vest. He looked trim and tough, not stocky and not lean.

Both he and Romaine hung their hats and went to clean up.

All three hands were seated at the table when Thane came in with his visitor. Thane presented him as Carson Lurie, and Monte stood up to shake his hand. Lurie gave him a handshake and a brief look, then went about the business of taking off his hat and coat. Thane took off his hat and coat, also, and the meal got under way.

Monte saw now that Lurie had a full head of brown, wavy hair, creased where the hat had ridden. He had blue eyes and a clear, almost rosy complexion. Although his face was filling out, he would probably pass for handsome with some women.

As usual, no one said much during the meal, but even without speaking, Farrell conveyed a dour, taciturn air. Just as Johnny Romaine could transmit cheerfulness in the way he laid his knife and fork on his plate, Farrell could express a total lack of humor by the way he dug a toothpick out of his shirt pocket. Lurie, on the other hand, expressed little at all. He ignored the hired men, his own included. Monte imagined the man had a separate cook for his own bunkhouse—so he wouldn't have to eat with his hired men, and so Dora wouldn't have to cook for them.

When dinner was ending, Horace announced and brought out an apple pie in a tin pie pan. It was a shallow pie, with the crusts shrunk in from the edges. Neither Farrell nor Lurie looked at it with much interest, but Horace seemed proud of it.

"You didn't give me much warning," he said, "but

I got 'er done. And the good part is, I only need to cut it six ways."

Thane had a delighted look on his face, as if someone were about to open a nice present, and Johnny wore the smile of any boy who was about to have some pie. Horace cut the pie and slid a piece onto each man's plate, then sat down to eat his portion.

Monte thought the crust was a bit doughy and the fruit a bit scarce, but any pie was worth a compliment, so he gave one. Johnny seconded it, and Thane gave a "Yessir" as Lurie and Farrell muttered agreement.

The men all drank another cup of coffee after that, but not much conversation came up. Thane and Johnny smoked, and Farrell picked at his teeth. Finally Lurie pushed himself back from the table, thanked Horace for the meal, and stood up. Farrell stood up also and mumbled a couple of words to Horace, who was sitting next to him. Then Lurie and Farrell said brief goodbyes and were gone.

In a few minutes, the thud of horse hooves sounded on the hard ground outside, and Thane looked around with a smile.

"Well, the comedy troupe is gone," Johnny said.

All four men laughed, and Monte looked at Johnny.

"They're always that way," said the smiling young puncher. "We're used to 'em."

The next morning, the Old Man told his boys that the two of them could ride out east together. "I don't want to sound the alarm," he said, "but Lurie told me it looked like someone had been pushing his cattle around. He's not sure but what he might be missing a few head, and he sent his man Weaver out on a line camp to keep an eye on things."

Monte thought Farrell would have been a good man for that job, until he realized Lurie might prefer to keep Farrell close by for protection.

Thane went on. "Just ride on out and keep your eyes open. Don't get crossed up with Elswick's men if you can avoid it, and stick together."

The boys nodded.

"And Monte, you've got a saddle gun, haven't you?"

"Yes, sir."

"Well, carry it. And Johnny, you do the same."

Monte looked at Johnny, who said, "Just a precaution. And we might see an elk."

Monte gave a short laugh. Elk down on the plains would be like prairie dogs in the high country timber. "All right," he said.

Morning lay crisp and frosty on the grassland as the two men rode out of the Three-Bar. The sun glinted on the horses' bits and cast a shine on the saddle leather. Monte pulled his hat forward to shade his eyes. He looked across at Johnny Romaine on his left, who had done the same. Johnny stood up in his stirrups, tugged on the inside of his woolly chaps, and sat down again. He looked over at Monte and smiled.

"I sure hope we don't see them fellas today," he said. "I wouldn't want to mix things up with them, and I sure wouldn't want to have to back down or run away."

"That's about how I feel," Monte answered back. "And I don't think Elswick'll be happy to see me again."

Johnny smiled as if he had thought of a good joke. "He doesn't have to like it. Now that you mention it, I hope he sees us. Maybe it'll give him indigestion."

They rode on in the clear morning, with the dry smell of sage and the warm smell of horses on the cold air. The sun rose quickly for the first half hour, but it did not melt the frost on the grass. Three antelope bolted about a quarter mile ahead, racing to the north and then wheeling in a white-and-tawny flash as they cut back to the southeast. Then the rangeland was still again, spreading out for miles toward the far-off buttes and mesas.

"Lot of country," Monte said.

"Yep," agreed Johnny. "You'd think there'd be enough for everyone." He frowned and looked at Monte. "I'm surprised we haven't seen any cattle yet."

At that moment they topped a little rise, and down below were half a dozen red cattle.

"Spoke too soon," Johnny said.

They rode down toward the cattle, which were grazing broadside to the sun. One of them looked up at the oncoming riders and bolted, taking the others along. The two punchers touched spurs to their horses and caught up with no trouble. Monte counted three cows and three calves. He could see the Three-Bar brand clearly on the left hip of each animal, so he slowed his horse and cut behind the animals. Headed east again, he slowed to a walk.

Johnny came up on his left, as before. "They all look all right. Three pair."

"Uh-huh."

"Well, that's what we came to see."

They rode on, raising cattle in small numbers from time to time. All of the Three-Bar cattle looked fine, and none of the other cattle looked as if they had been tampered with.

"Whose cattle are these white-face?" Monte asked.

"Those are Lurie's. That's his Circle-L brand."

Monte nodded. "And what's Elswick's?"

"The Half-Diamond-E we've been seein'."

"That's what I thought. His cattle don't look too bad, either."

"No, they don't."

Monte looked again at the Circle-L brand. "I think the Three-Bar would be easier to change than this one."

"That's true. But you'll notice Elswick runs different breeds, so he can send a mixed bunch, say, to someone who butchers for a ditch crew or a railroad crew, and no one inspects a brand there."

"Uh-huh."

"And for all we know, he might have a second brand in his back pocket that he uses for shipping deals."

"Like a Box-Eight," Monte said.

Johnny laughed. "Yeah. He could steal every one of the Old Man's cattle with that. He might have somethin', anyway, if cattle are disappearin' in his neighborhood."

They rode onward a few more miles, then turned

north. A slight breeze had picked up and was blowing in their faces. Johnny put his bandanna up to cover his nose and mouth, then took it down again. The two riders ducked their heads and moved forward into the breeze.

About half an hour later, Monte thought he smelled smoke. He asked Johnny, who lifted his head, sniffed, and nodded. They put their horses into a fast walk and moved on. About a quarter of a mile farther, they heard the bawling of a calf. The two riders looked at each other. Monte was about to spur his horse into a lope when a thought crossed his mind. He reined back on his horse.

"We could be ridin' into a bellyful of lead," he said in a low voice. "Let's split up and come at it on two sides."

Johnny nodded, and the two of them moved off separately in a walk.

They found the calf by itself in a little draw that ran east and west. Monte rode around to Johnny's side of the draw, and then the two of them went down together to take a look. It was a red Durham calf lying on its right side, with a Three-Bar brand showing on its left hip. It was a small calf for this time of year, but it was still over two hundred pounds. Its rear hocks were tied to the front left ankle, and it raised its head as the two riders approached.

It all looked plain to Monte. The calf wasn't slick. It had been branded in the spring and had begun to hair over. Someone must have thought he could change the brand and move the animal out. Whoever it was had been in a hurry; he had left the pig-

John D. Nesbitt

gin' string on the calf and had left a little sagebrush branding fire.

"I wonder where its mother is," Monte said as he stepped down from his horse.

Johnny, who had also dismounted, reached down and pulled the piggin' string loose. The calf scrambled to its feet and trotted away. "Hard to say. Maybe they drove this calf quite a ways, or maybe it's lost its mother and was off by itself." Johnny ran the string through his hands and studied it. "You know, there's some fellas would lame or kill a cow just to be able to brand a calf, but that would more likely happen if the calf was slick.

"Uh-huh. And this one was branded plain as day."

"Sure was. Well, that's news for the Old Man."

After the two punchers had kicked out the fire, they decided to see if they could find the calf and therefore see if it had a mother. They rode circles for the next hour, and they saw no Three-Bar cattle at all.

"They must have brought him quite a ways," Johnny said. "No tellin' where he hightailed it back to."

Monte looked around at the wide country. "No, but I bet he's happy to be free."

70

Chapter Five

By midday they had covered quite a bit of country without pushing the horses. After finding the calf, they had ridden on north a ways farther, then curved back around to the west and south and back east again—all without crossing the main trail that Monte had taken into town a few days earlier. With Lurie's place and Thane's to the west of that trail, and Elswick's to the east, Monte wondered if the trail served as an unofficial boundary line, even though it crossed open range as he had confirmed.

Monte imagined that the trail lay just a little ways to the east of the spot where they stopped for a midday rest. They sat in the lee of a south-facing knoll, out of the wind and in the sun. Monte held the horses' reins while Johnny rolled himself a cigarette. Since finding the calf tied up they had found nothing else out of the ordinary, and they had seen no other riders. Johnny motioned with his head toward his saddle, where he had tied the piggin' string. It was a piece of hemp rope about four feet long and less than half an inch thick, and it hung in three coils.

"I sure wonder whose string that is," he said. "You know, Thrall chews tobacco. I bet a top-notch detective could find out if there was any tobacco slobber on it."

Monte pictured Thrall holding the coils of the piggin' string in his mouth while he swung his rope, the way a lot of riders did when they roped a calf by themselves. "I wouldn't be surprised," he said.

Johnny put a thoughtful look on his face as he smoked his cigarette. "I just thought of someone else we could ask."

"Who's that?"

"A couple of fellas that have a meat-huntin' camp out here."

"What kind of meat?" As far as Monte knew, there were no buffalo left to speak of.

"Antelope," said Johnny with a smile. "They go out and shoot a wagonload, and then they take it into town to old Wheeler. He packs it in salt brine, in barrels, and ships it out."

"Do they make any money at that?"

"Oh, a little bit, I suppose. It's somethin' to be doin'. A little later on, they'll hunt wolves and coyotes, and do some trappin' on through the winter."

Monte nodded. Cold weather was the time to hunt meat and trap furs. "What do they do in the summer?"

"Oh, they punch cows over on a ranch by Castle

Butte. They move down about this far to hunt meat, and then they trap their way back."

Monte wrinkled his nose. He had met men who trapped all winter and took on a pretty strong smell. They got to where they couldn't smell themselves. An antelope camp wouldn't be so bad, and it would be less likely to have fleas and ticks. "We could drop by," he said.

"Let's do that. You ought to get to know 'em, anyway." Johnny looked at the sun and smiled. "We ought to get there about in time for dinner."

After he finished his cigarette and stomped it out, Johnny led the way east, across the main trail, and then veered north and east. "These boys are named Riggs," he said. "They're brothers. They should be camped on a creek up ahead here."

Before long the two riders came to a creek that flowed east. After crossing it, they followed it for nearly a mile until a camp came into view. About a quarter mile from the camp they stopped the horses to let them relieve themselves; then they rode on in slowly so as not to raise much dust.

Johnny called out and waved as two men stood up. They waved, and one of them took a few steps forward as the other crouched again by the firelight.

Drawing closer, Monte could see that the man was a young fellow about Johnny's age. He wore a beard, as did the other young man by the fire.

Johnny swung down from the saddle with his spurs jingling as he hit the ground. He said, "How d'ye do, Earl?" as he shook the man's hand. "Who's that scout you got with you there? Do I know this lad? Hello, George."

Earl looked up at Monte, who hadn't presumed to dismount since he hadn't met the host yet. "Pile off, and pick a bone with us."

Monte swung down and was introduced to the Riggs brothers. Earl looked as if he might be a year or two older than George, but they seemed close in age and spirit. They wore dirty work shirts and canvas trousers, but they did not smell bad. Their camp was neat, consisting of a canvas-covered wagon draped with half a dozen carcasses on the shady side, a white canvas wall tent, a kitchen laid out on the ground, and two horses picketed a ways from camp.

The brothers grinned as they urged their visitors to eat with them.

"What's for grub?" asked Johnny, sniffing the air.

"Salt pork and beans," answered George, returning to the fire pit and kneeling.

Earl turned to Monte. "You're welcome to some antelope steak, but we don't care to eat it when we've been butcherin' it all day."

"No, that's fine. Whatever you've got handy."

Earl helped Johnny put the horses out to picket, and then the four men sat down to eat. George uncovered a Dutch oven of biscuits and handed out two apiece, and each man served up a tin plate of beans. They ate without talking much, as was the habit on the range.

After everyone had eaten two servings, Johnny took out the makin's, rolled himself a cigarette, and tossed the bag to Earl. He troughed a paper, shook some tobacco into it, and tossed the bag to his brother.

When everyone had lit up, Earl asked, "Did you boys come out to hunt? I notice you brought your smoke poles."

"Nah," said Johnny. "We're out checkin' on things."

"See anything?"

"Not much, but we did find a calf tied up like someone wanted to change his name."

Earl cocked his head. "Whereabouts?"

Johnny pointed backward with his thumb. "West of here a couple of miles, and a little bit south."

"Hmm." Earl looked at his brother and then back at the Three-Bar riders. "We sure haven't seen anything."

George spoke up. "We'll keep an eye out, though."

"That would help," Johnny said. "How long you think you'll be here?"

"Oh, a couple more days, probably. Then we'll move on up to Wagon Creek." Earl looked at Monte. "That's the next one north of here."

Monte motioned with his head. "What's this one called?"

"Arrow Creek."

Johnny looked over at George. "Who's been killin' all the goats—you or your brother?"

George smiled. "Oh, it's been about half and half. I miss half of mine, and he misses half of his."

"Looks like you've done all right," Monte said.

"Oh, yeah," George answered. "We killed those this morning."

"Doin' all right, then," said Johnny.

"Oh, yeah. We can't complain, can we, Earl?"

"Oh, no."

"Well, that's good," said Johnny. He paused for a long drag on his cigarette and then looked at Earl. "Do you know of anyone sellin' much fresh beef?"

Earl rubbed his face and pushed his hat up. "No, not offhand. They're not butcherin' calves, are they?"

"No, but they might have made beefsteak out of his mother. I don't know. The little calf got away before we could see. But it's just another angle."

The talk went on from there, jolly and full of jokes, about nesters and other loose operators who ate too much beef and made rawhide lariats to use up the evidence. Then the talk went to the weather, which it always did, and then to the subject of work. After a second cigarette, Johnny said he needed to get home to milk the cow and feed the chickens, which was another nester joke.

As the two riders mounted up and made ready to leave, Earl told them to come back anytime. "Come on out to shoot," he said. "This would give you some good practice."

Then they said "So long" all the way around, and the two riders moved out of camp.

"Those are good boys," Johnny said when they had ridden out a ways.

"Uh-huh. Seemed like it to me."

"They stay out of things, and no one bothers 'em. But if they see somethin' that's not right, they'll tell us about it. They don't like this crooked stuff any better than the rest of us do."

*   *   *

The next day being Sunday, Monte and Johnny had a day off. During roundup and shipping there was no observance of Sunday, but when work was not pressing, most ranches gave the hands some free time on Sunday. A ride to town seemed to be in order today, so the boys got cleaned up. Monte took a bath, shaved his face, and trimmed his mustache, as did Johnny. As they were leaving the bunkhouse, spruced up and wearing clean shirts, Monte noticed that Johnny was wearing the horsehair watch chain. He had no doubt that Johnny also had the elk ivories in his vest pocket.

Johnny was in a happy mood as they rode across country. When they came to the edge of town, he brushed off his sleeves and used his hand to comb down his mustache.

"Say, Monte," he began. "There's a girl I like to go see, if you don't mind bein' on your own for a little while."

Monte, who had his own ideas about a girl and who had been afraid he might have to go to the saloon first just to be sociable, said, "That's fine. You can look for me when you get free. I'll be easy to find."

"All right." Johnny turned left on a side street and rode away.

Monte rode straight for the café. When he walked in, he saw two cowpunchers sitting at the table where he and Johnny had sat. He nodded to them and walked to the last table on his right, where he took off his coat and sat with his back to the kitchen. As he was taking off his hat, Ramona appeared on his right.

She was smiling as before, and he felt himself go

soft at the sight of her dark eyes and smooth, tan skin.

"So you came back," she said.

"Yeah, but I'm afraid to ask if there's any pie."

"Oh, no," she said. "It never lasts more than two days."

"Well, then I'll just have coffee."

"Are you sure?"

He smiled and said, "Yeah, for right now."

"All right."

As she turned and walked away, he noticed she was wearing a dark blue wool dress that went all the way to her ankles. He liked her walk as before, and he liked her dark hair as it lay in waves on her shoulders.

She came back with his coffee and set it down, pausing to exchange smiles before she moved on to the other table. The two men were getting up to leave. The three of them exchanged pleasant talk, which Monte did not try to hear, and then the men left.

Ramona came back to his table. "Well, how do you like working for Mr. Thane?"

"Just fine. He's a good boss, and Johnny's a good hand to work with." Then, to save her a question, he said, "Johnny rode in with me, but he's busy right now. He'll probably come in later."

She was about to speak again when the bell tinkled and the front door opened. A man in a slouch hat and overcoat came in, and looking at the two people in back, he walked to the rear of the café and stood by the table next to Monte's. He was a man of middle height, and as he took off the heavy wool overcoat, Monte saw that he was dressed in normal clothes for cattle country but didn't look like a cowpuncher. He looked soft, and his clothes did not look weathered. He gave Monte a glance and sat with his back to the door.

He ordered coffee also, and as soon as Ramona was gone, he looked across at Monte. "Gettin' to be that time of year, isn't it?"

"Sure is."

"No use tryin' to second-guess the weather, though."

"That's for sure."

"That first storm came as a real surprise, and now when you think it's gonna snow, it doesn't."

"Uh-huh."

"I think the worst of it is that durn wind."

"It does blow."

"Doesn't it, though? And I'll tell you what, it drives some people crazy."

"I've heard that."

"Uh-huh. I believe it. Me, I can live with it."

Ramona brought his coffee and set it down.

"Thanks, hon."

"Anything else?" she asked.

"Not right now," he said, "but if I think of somethin' I'll whistle."

Ramona walked back into the kitchen and out of sight.

"I'll tell ya," the man went on, "I sat in a cabin for ten days, just out of Miles City, and listened to that wind whine and whine. The snow wasn't so bad. It was the drifts afterwards that made it hard to get anywhere."

"Uh-huh."

"But I don't suppose I'm tellin' you anything. You look like you've seen some weather."

"I've seen some."

"Do you work hereabouts, or are you passin' through?"

"I work at the Three-Bar, southwest of here. And yourself?"

"I just got here. I came through Douglas."

"Uh-huh."

The man sipped his coffee. "Say, I hate to have to shout. Do you mind if I join you?"

As it was the middle of the day, Monte thought the man might be moving along in a little while, so he said, "Not at all. Come on over."

The man transferred his overcoat and coffee, then leaned over and extended his hand. "Name's Conde. Art Conde."

"Pleased to meet you," said Monte as he rose from his chair. "Monte Casteel."

The man had a firm handshake, although his chest and shoulders looked slack. He had wide, brown eyes and a soft face, ending in a soft chin with sparse stubble on it. He looked to be about Monte's age or a little older.

"Do you think they need any more help on your ranch?" he asked.

"I couldn't say, but I doubt it. The Old Man usually carries just one hand on through the winter, and he's got two right now."

"Any others you know of that might could use a hand?"

"I don't really know any of 'em well enough to say."

"Uh-huh. Well, I'll tell you, my specialty is trainin' horses." He held up his hands. "Don't get me wrong. I'm not a bronc rider. I do a lot of my work from the ground. I can halter break, saddle break, harness break, put a finish on a horse if it hasn't been ruined by rough riding . . . Excuse me, I hope I didn't say something. Are you a horse breaker?"

"No, not so much. Go ahead."

"Well, as I was sayin', I could use a little work. Ceres and Bacchus do not come free."

"What's that?"

"The grain and the grape. It's cost me nearly every cent I had just to get this far from Great Falls."

"I thought you said Miles City."

Conde looked straight at Monte. "Oh, I did. But I was in Miles City at this time last year. That's when I got snowed in. But I'm comin' from Great Falls now."

"Well, you could ask around. I think the Old Man's gonna have us cuttin' logs, but I don't know what the others are doin'."

"I like to stick with my trade when I can," said Conde, giving a straight look again with his wide, brown eyes.

"Uh-huh."

"And as much as I hate to, I think I might have to sell one of my horses."

Now everything fit into place, Monte thought. The man was a horse trader.

"That's a hard sale right now," Monte said. "Everyone's done with roundup work till spring, so every ranch has got the pick of the horse herd for winter work."

"Well, not everyone's a cattleman," Conde said. "There's freighters and packers and regular travelers. I've got a horse that's gentle to ride and packs like a mule."

Ramona appeared at the kitchen doorway and then vanished.

"That's a good kind of horse," said Monte, wishing the man would shut up and leave.

"Easy keeper," Conde went on. "Got a heart of gold."

"Uh-huh."

"You ought to look at him."

"I don't really need a horse. I ride ranch horses, and I've got one of my own when I need him." He looked to see if Ramona was back at the doorway, but she wasn't.

"Hell, take a look at him. You could turn around and sell him and damn near double your money."

Monte couldn't see any other way of getting rid of the man, so he said, "All right. I'll take a look at him, but I'm really not in the market for another horse."

Ramona came to the doorway as the men stood up.

Monte looked at her and winked as he said, "We'll be back in a couple of minutes. He wants to show me a horse."

She smiled and nodded.

Out in the street, Conde led the way to a sorrel horse that stood next to a larger dun. The sorrel had a small pack on its back and was tied with a lead rope from its halter to the hitch rail. It was a medium-sized horse, about fourteen hands high and sturdy-looking.

"No brands. Clean bill of sale." Conde pulled the lead rope loose from its knot and patted the horse on the left front shoulder. He pulled loose the cinches on the pack, which was a padded leather packsaddle with panniers and no breeching, and slid the whole pack off together and into the street. "Plumb gentle," he said. Then he put both hands on the horse's withers and vaulted up onto the horse's back. He moved the horse out from the rail and down the street, swung it around, loped it back to Monte's left, swung it around again, and brought it back at a quick walk. He slid off the horse's back and handed the lead rope toward Monte. "Give 'im a try."

"Nah, that's all right. I can see he's not lame."

"And plumb gentle. A kid could ride him, or a lady."

"Uh-huh."

"Hell, for twenty dollars you'd be practically stealin' him. And you could damn near double your money if you wanted."

Monte glanced at the window of the café and saw Ramona looking out at them. "If you sell this horse," he said, "how will you carry your pack?"

"Don't worry about that. This big bastard could carry me an' two fat Indians if I wanted him to."

Monte smiled but said nothing. He had seen both sides of the horse and had verified that it had no brands. "This horse been to the mountains?" he asked.

"Born and raised there. He'll pack out anything you shoot, as long as it's dead."

"I imagine." Monte pushed out his lower lip and thought for a moment.

"How about it? Half a month's wages is all."

Monte knew he had a twenty-dollar gold piece snug in his pocket. It was half a month's wages at his last job, anyway. "Clean bill of sale?" he asked.

"You bet. The one I'm carryin', and one from me to you."

"All right. I'll take it."

Back inside, Conde drank the rest of his coffee as he wrote out and dated the bill of sale. Then he took the twenty-dollar gold piece and stood up. He reached into his pocket and brought out a two-bit piece, looked at it, and hesitated.

"That's all right," Monte said. "I'll take care of the coffee."

Conde looked at him. "Well, maybe I'll be able to return the favor someday."

"Maybe you will." Monte stood up and shook hands. "Maybe we'll meet again, somewhere on down the trail."

Conde smiled. "I hope so." Then, putting on his overcoat and tipping his hat, he said, "May that pony serve you well and never stumble."

Monte remained standing. He watched as the man walked out of the café, lifted the leather pack onto the swells of his saddle, sprang up onto the back of the big bastard dun, and rode away.

He turned, smiling, and saw Ramona standing a

few feet away. He liked the feeling of being that close to her, and he didn't like having lost so much time with Conde.

"I just bought an extra horse," he said. "You don't happen to need one, do you?"

"No," she said, shaking her head. "I've got one I hardly ever ride." After a pause she gave him an inquisitive look and said, "Did you buy it for any special reason?"

He felt comfortable with her tone. It gave him a feeling of familiarity, as if she knew him well enough to ask him a casual question. "Not really," he said, feeling a little sheepish. "I guess it'll come in handy if and when I get ready to leave."

"Do you expect to leave pretty soon?"

He looked at her, feeling again a softness as he saw her honey skin and the friendliness in her dark eyes. He felt as if he had known her for a long while. "I'm not in any hurry. I just had it in my head that I wanted to see the mountains further west, or I wouldn't even be thinking that much about leaving."

"You haven't been there before?"

"No," he said. "It's just an idea." Then, thinking there might be something else to her question, he said, "I've never been there, and I don't know anyone out there. It's just something I want to do. I've lived in Wyoming all my life, and I haven't seen much of it."

"That's good, to see new places."

He wondered if she meant the comment to refer to herself as well, for having come here with Flynn or even for wanting to get out. "Uh-huh," he said. "There's lots out there to see."

They had been standing near each other for a couple of minutes, and although he liked the sensation, he thought it might look curious if someone should happen to come in. "Well," he said, "I suppose I could sit back down."

She surprised him with a question. "Do you want to see my horse?"

He hesitated for a second, certain he had heard her correctly but not sure of her purpose. Given the tone of the moment, he did not think she was trying to sell him another horse. "I suppose so," he said, thinking it would at least give him a little more time with her. He looked around at the café. "Can you just leave this place like this?"

"For a few minutes. It won't hurt anything."

Monte had put on his coat when she came back from the kitchen wearing hers, a long overcoat of coarse gray wool.

"Is it in the stable?" he asked as they stepped outside.

"Yes. Sometimes I think I should sell it, because all I do is pay every month to keep it there."

"Uh-huh." Monte thought about offering her his arm, but he saw she had her hands in her coat pockets.

"But I keep it. I tell myself I might need it." She looked at him. "I think it helps me feel better, to know I have it there."

"Oh. Uh-huh." He tried to imagine how it might be with her, a woman by herself in a small town off the main route. Keeping a horse might give her a peace of mind, a sense that she could leave if she felt she had to.

Ramona spoke with the stable man and led Monte through the stable, past the place where he had spent the night. She pointed out a bay horse that shared a pen with two other horses. "That's him."

The pen, a small corral, lay in back of the stable and led into a wide stall where the horses could feed at a manger. The horses in the pen were all gentle, so Monte had no trouble separating Ramona's horse, bringing it into the stall, and shutting out the others.

It was a nice-looking horse, even though it hadn't seen much use of late. It was about the same size as the sorrel that Monte had just bought. Its dark mane and tail were matted and uncombed, and the horse looked out of shape from spending so much time in a pen. It looked like a bartender's horse, he thought, but a little care and exercise could bring out its good features.

Monte stood inside the stall with the horse as Ramona stood on the other side of the gate, in the alleyway of the stable.

"Did you want me to do anything with him?" he asked.

"Not necessarily. I just thought you could take a look at him."

"You mean, to give you an opinion? Like whether you should keep him or sell him?"

"I guess so. Just to tell me if he's any good."

"He looks all right to me. He just needs to be combed out and exercised."

"I know he needs that."

Monte looked at Ramona. "It's not something I could do all at once, in five minutes. But I could do a little now, if you wanted."

"That would be nice, but I wasn't asking you to do it."

"That's all right," he said, opening the gate and stepping into the alleyway with her. "I can find a halter and a brush and a comb, and I can do a little bit." He paused. "You probably need to get back to your café, don't you?"

She glanced in that general direction, then twitched her nose as she shook her head. "I can stay here for a few minutes."

Monte found the halter, brush, and comb without any trouble. He had combed out plenty of range horses that had been out all winter, so this would be an easy job. He tied up the horse inside the stall, brushed it down, and started combing out the tangles in the black mane. He took it a little at a time, pulling the steel comb through the narrow strands. The horse gave no trouble, flinching from time to time but not fighting back.

"We'll get a little bit done today," he said. "Then maybe I could do some more next time, if you wanted."

She was standing on the other side of the gate, but he felt as if she were standing right next to him as her voice came over. "I didn't mean to ask you to do that much. I just wanted to know what you thought."

"Oh, that's all right. I like this kind of work." He smiled as his eyes met hers, and he felt a nervousness. It was the good kind of nervousness, the kind a fellow had with a pretty girl. It gave him a touch of courage. "Besides," he said, "I can't think of anyone else I'd rather be doing this for."

Her eyes sparkled as she said, "That's good."

Chapter Six

The wind blew cold from the north. Monte and his pal Johnny rode east as they had done two days earlier. When they were a few miles out they began riding circles—splitting up, riding out and around, circling back, and meeting up. They had orders from Thane to cover the country thoroughly and see if anything else looked suspicious.

When they were within a mile of the main north-south trail, by Monte's estimation, they began working southward and parallel to the trail. Again, it seemed as if the trail worked as a sort of boundary. Although they had crossed it to visit the Riggs brothers, they did not cross it for the purposes of checking cattle. Monte knew that the cattle didn't care about a line like that, not any more than antelope did, so he finally asked Johnny.

"By the Old Man's thinkin', it's easier to stay out

of trouble if we do our lookin' on this side of the trail. It's a good bet that our cattle drift on over east—in fact, we saw some when we went over there the other day—and the farther they go, the more likely they are to fall into mischief. But if we find somethin' out of square over on this side, then we'll have an idea of how far west someone is comin' to cause trouble."

They had their backs to the wind now, and Monte watched a tumbleweed pass them by on the left. Then he turned to the right to look at Johnny.

"Not to mention any names," Monte said, "but if someone's goin' out of his way to throw a wide loop when he could do it closer to home, then he must be pushin' for trouble."

"That's true. For all we know, they could've seen us turn north the other day and then quick got out ahead of us and set that up."

"Uh-huh. That's one possibility. The other is that it was exactly the way it looked to us when we rode onto it."

Johnny spit off to his right. "Yep. That's for sure."

They worked the range south for a couple of hours, then buttonhooked back to the west and started working north. At midday they ate a lunch of biscuits and cold meat. When Horace had handed them the food in a cloth bag that morning, Monte knew they were in for an all-day ride. He imagined they were at the far end of the ride, but he didn't ask. He didn't like to ask a lot of questions, since that was a tenderfoot thing to do and most of the questions got answered sooner or later anyway. Moreover, Johnny didn't always seem to have a definite plan. It wasn't that the kid didn't think, because it looked as if he usually was thinking, but he seemed to be the type of person who kept things open by not working out a detailed plan.

The way Monte saw it, Thane gave the orders and Johnny knew how to carry them out. Monte was making thirty a month to do what he was told and to stay out of trouble. As time went on and he knew the ranch better, he might take on a little more initiative, but for the time being they went and stopped where Johnny took them.

Johnny ground out the snipe of his cigarette and took a drink from his canteen. "I suppose we might as well put our noses back into the wind," he said. Then he turned and grinned. "But it beats building an icehouse, doesn't it?"

Monte smiled back. "We might end up doing that, too."

Then the two of them mounted their horses and rode face into the cold wind.

They rode as before, circling out and around and joining up, then repeating the pattern. Monte saw cattle from time to time, usually down in a protected spot out of the wind. Nothing seemed out of the ordinary. At about midafternoon they came to the place where they had found the calf tied up. It looked like any other draw, with the exception of a little black spot where they had put out the fire. They rode down through the draw, back up onto the plain, and onward.

About an hour later, Johnny said, "We ought to be able to find Weaver's line camp out here somewhere."

Monte recalled the name. "That's Lurie's man, isn't it?"

Johnny yawned and said, "Uh-huh."

They found Weaver's camp at the edge of a small, east-flowing creek that barely ran a trickle. The camp was visible from a ways off, as it consisted of a white, pyramid-shaped sleeping tent and a smoking campfire. Weaver had set his camp downstream from a patch of box elder trees, now leafless. The tent was north of the creek and south of a little bluff that would give some protection from the wind. Between the tent and the creek, the fire was blazing. Monte saw a horse, stripped and picketed, about a hundred yards out from the camp, but he did not see a man. Seeing only one horse, he imagined Lurie's outfit had packed the camp out and had then left the outrider alone.

A couple of hundred feet from the campfire, Johnny called out. After no answer he called again. A man appeared at the tent flap, crouching, and stepped out.

"Come on in," he called.

As the riders came in closer, Monte saw a saddle near the fire and a rifle propped up on a small stack of logs.

"Get off and visit," said the man. He jerked his thumb back over his shoulder. "I was in there changin' socks."

The two riders swung down from their horses, and Monte met the man of the camp, who introduced himself as Mort Weaver.

The first thing Monte noticed, even from a distance, was the man's long, bushy mustache, which

John D. Nesbitt

was of a dusty blond color like his hair. He had about a week's stubble on his face, as well. Closer up, Monte noticed the man's eyes were bloodshot. His face looked relaxed, and Monte guessed he had had something to drink.

"Siddown, siddown," Weaver said. "Put your horses out for a little while. You're the first company I've had in a week, and you're not gonna run off on me that quick."

Monte put the horses out to graze. He picketed them separately, fifty feet apart, and hung their bridles on their saddle horns as he loosened the cinches. He got back to the camp as Johnny was finishing the story about the calf they had found. Monte sat down on the ground with the other two men.

"Sons a bitches," said Weaver, throwing a stem of grass at the fire. "All these cattlemen are alike. Ten, twenty years ago, they all mavericked till hell wouldn't have it. Paid their punchers extra to do it, and then when they got to be mucky-mucks they decided they wanted to go after the little operators, and they used rustlin' as an excuse. Now, when there's some real rustlin' goin' on, where the hell are they? Where's the law? Uh?"

"You know where the sheriff is. He's gettin' his guts purged. But he'll be back."

"Sure. And meanwhile this son of a bitch Elswick can steal anything he wants."

Weaver's voice was loud, and Monte winced.

"We don't know for sure what's goin' on," Johnny said, "but we need to stick together on this until we find out."

"It's all goin' to hell, that's what." Weaver leaned over and pulled a bottle from underneath his saddle. "You got the railroads, the homesteaders, and the ditch projects—" He pulled the cork out with a squeak and offered the bottle to each of his guests, who declined. He held the bottle in front of him and swayed a little before he spoke again. "And then you got these bigwigs that think they can still run everything." He took a drink. "Isn't that right?"

No one answered. Weaver put the cork back into the bottleneck and pressed it with his right thumb. "Hell with all of 'em," he said. "If it all goes to hell, maybe the little man'll have a chance again."

"Who knows," Johnny said.

"I tried," Weaver went on. "I took up some land, but I couldn't make a go of it. They don't give you a chance. You try to get up, and they knock you down. And when you're down, they kick you."

"Have you got a place around here?" Johnny asked.

"No, way over west. But I'm pullin' out. I just needed more of a stake, so that's why I'm workin' here."

Weaver reached into his overcoat and brought out his makin's. Johnny brought out his, and the two of them rolled smokes. Weaver's eyelids drooped. He seemed to be studying his work, but he did a sloppy job of it. When he got it licked he stuck the cigarette in his mouth and took a light off of Johnny's match.

"Well," he said, "if you boys don't want any firewater, I'd better make some coffee."

"Finish your cigarette," Monte said. "We're in no

hurry." He looked at the sun, which was off in the west by now. "I'll go get some firewood, so we don't run you out of it."

Monte rose to his feet and walked upstream to the clump of box elder trees. He found a couple of dead branches on the ground and began breaking them into firewood length. He could not hear anything from the camp except the general drone of human speech.

As he was walking back to the camp with an armload of sticks, he saw two riders coming from the east. One of them looked like Thrall, but he could not place the other one. The man didn't have the shape of either Pool or Elswick.

"Looks like company," he said, setting down the firewood.

Weaver looked off to the east, then back at his rifle.

Johnny craned his neck and looked too. "Looks like Thrall," he said. "And someone else."

"Let 'em come," Weaver said. "This is an open camp." He slipped the bottle back in its place and stood up at the same time as Johnny did.

The riders came on in, halloing the camp and getting the holler back. It wasn't until they were within forty yards that Monte recognized the second rider as Conde. He didn't recognize the man sooner because he didn't expect to see him with Thrall. It looked as if Conde had found a job; it also looked as if he'd gotten into more than he might have expected.

Weaver invited the men to come in and step down, which they did. Thrall and Weaver apparently already knew each other, so the only stranger was Conde. As introductions were being made, Conde mentioned that he and Monte had already met.

Thrall spoke in his rough voice. "Where do you know him from?"

"That's who I sold the horse to. In town."

Thrall looked at Monte and then at Weaver, where he let his glance rest. He seemed to be sizing him up. Then he turned to Conde and told him to take the horses and tie them up in the trees.

Monte took a look at Thrall. The man was not tall—maybe an inch shorter than Conde. He was wearing shotgun chaps with pockets on the front, which made him look even stockier than before. He was wearing the same coat and hat as he had on the earlier meeting, and if he had shaved in the meanwhile it had been a few days. He reached into his coat pocket, brought out a leather pouch, and opened the drawstring. With his meaty right thumb and forefinger he pulled out a stringy hunk of tobacco and pushed it into his mouth.

Conde came back to the camp with his unoffending air. His wide brown eyes and soft chin went up and down as he nodded to Weaver and the Three-Bar riders.

"I was just gonna get some coffee goin'," Weaver said. "Have a seat."

Everyone sat down but Weaver. He went through the laborious task of putting a pot of coffee together and onto the fire, which had burned down to a good bed of coals. Then he sat down and said, "There's firewater for anyone that wants it."

Conde's face lifted and brightened until Thrall said, "Nah." Conde took out a tin cigarette case, opened it, and picked out a tailor-made cigarette. Weaver reached into the fire pit and pulled out a stub of a stick with a glowing end, then held it for Conde to light his cigarette.

"Thanks," said Conde.

Weaver winked and nodded.

Silence hung in the air for a moment until Johnny looked at Thrall and said, "Cattle look pretty good over our way. How about yours?"

"All right. They seem to be crowdin' over on our better grass, but other'n that, the range looks all right."

Monte could see Conde's eyes moving back and forth between the two men speaking.

Thrall's gravelly voice sounded again. "We came over here to see who had a fire."

Weaver looked up from staring at the coals. "I guess you found out."

"I guess I did. We saw the smoke a mile away, and we was wonderin' who was so damn stupid. A big fire, in this wind, and you'll have this whole range burned off."

"I was keepin' an eye on it," Weaver said.

Monte glanced at Johnny, who flicked his eyebrows.

"The hell," came Thrall's voice again. "You're drunk. You could burn up the whole country."

"Oh, piss on you," Weaver said. "This is my camp. I don't need you comin' in tellin' me how to do things."

Thrall sulked for a second and then said, "Someone ought to."

"Well, it doesn't need to be you." Weaver leaned over to pull out his bottle again, and both Thrall and Conde watched him. Weaver had an impudent look on his face as he turned back around and said, "Or anyone else from your outfit."

Monte was sure that Thrall had come to pick a fight and was pushing right into it.

"What's wrong with my outfit?"

Weaver pulled the cork out with a squeak, and with his head wavering he said, "Ask anyone on the Badwater."

Thrall's chest went up as he flinched back. "I wouldn't talk about somethin' I didn't know anythin' about," he said, and a few flecks of spit flew.

Weaver wiped off the mouth of his bottle and took a drink. "You were there too. You know what kind of a tinhorn you work for. Try to take another man's wife, and then run out on her." Weaver pushed the cork back into the bottle and looked up. "And you can't call me a liar. You know that."

Thrall was seething. "I do. I do call you a liar. What about that?" Thrall put his right fist on the ground and leaned toward Weaver.

No one could misunderstand the challenge.

"Oh, hell," Weaver went on. "I'm too drunk to fight, but I'm not afraid of you, or your tinhorn boss, or any of his cheap gunmen that he brings in."

Monte, cringing at the allusion to Pool, looked at

Conde, who was still taking it all in as if it were a poker game.

Using his right arm as a post, Thrall rose up in a pivot, brought his heavy left hand around, and slapped it against Weaver's right cheekbone. Weaver's hat flew off, and he fell back on his elbow.

Monte was on his feet now and moving around to stand between Weaver and Thrall. Looking down, he could see a bald spot on the back of Weaver's head. He reached down and handed the man his hat, then turned to look at Thrall.

"He's drunk, Thrall. Leave him alone."

Thrall's voice came out of his throat. "It's drunk talk that gets a man in trouble." Thrall stood up. "Just like buttin' in."

Monte could feel his stomach tightening now. Thrall was still spoiling for a fight. "I just said he was drunk. You can come back and pick a fight with him when he's—"

Thrall came up with both hands and gave Monte a powerful shove backward.

Monte landed on his rear and looked up. Thrall was taking off his coat. He tossed it on the ground, then tossed his gun and hat onto that. Elswick must have told him not to do any shooting, Monte thought. That would be Pool's game.

Monte came to his feet and took off his own coat, hat, and gun. He saw Thrall with his head leaning forward, the thick head with bristly hair and a heavy brow. The two hands hung low and doubled up, like boxing gloves.

Monte took two steps in and landed a left jab on Thrall's jaw, then stepped back as Thrall's right meat hook came across in front of his nose. He stepped in again with a left and a right on Thrall's cheekbones, but he couldn't budge him. Thrall came up with a right bear-paw and clapped Monte behind the ear, then dug his fingers into the base of Monte's skull and pulled him forward. Monte could smell the strong odor of body sweat, and he couldn't aim a punch with his head being pulled down. He felt Thrall's other hand clap the right side of his head, so he dropped to one knee, ducked his head out of Thrall's grasp, and came up holding Thrall's left leg out by the bootheel. Thrall could not reach him now, but rather had to hop on his right heel to keep his balance. Then Monte gave a jerk and a twist to the boot, and Thrall showed a look of surprise as he fell on his butt.

Thrall was up again, sweating now. Monte's right fist glanced off the slick forehead. Thrall swung again, but again he missed as Monte moved away. Monte could tell that Thrall was more of a mauler than a boxer, and he knew he had to stay away from those powerful arms. He stung Thrall again with a left jab to the mouth, then landed a good blow to the side of Thrall's head just in front of the ear. Thrall clubbed Monte once on the left side, and then Monte came back with two more like before. Thrall went woozy and let his guard down, and Monte knocked him down with a third punch to the side of his head.

Monte stood back as Thrall came up to his hands and knees. The other three men were up on their feet and standing by. Monte could see in a glance that Johnny Romaine was ready if Thrall went for his gun. Monte waited as Thrall crouched on the ground, then moved on all fours to the spot where he had tossed his coat. He put the hat on his head and the gun in his holster, then stood up with the coat as he kept his back to Monte. He looked around to his right and said, in his gravelly voice, "Go get the horses."

Conde made haste without a word.

Thrall walked a few paces away from the camp, hooked the tobacco out of his mouth and flung it on the ground, and put his hands on his knees. Bringing up a deep cough, he spit on the ground.

Conde came back riding one horse and leading the other. Still with his noncommittal air, he nodded to the other three men. Thrall pulled himself into the saddle and swung the horse away from the camp, and the two men rode away.

Weaver seemed to have sobered up a little. "I think maybe I said too much," he said. "Those son a bitches'll want to come back and get me in the middle of the night."

"I don't think so," Johnny said. He looked at Monte. "You let him have it pretty good."

Monte shrugged. "I rang his bell all right, but Weaver said some things that won't set well if they get repeated."

Johnny looked at Weaver. "Look here," he said. "Why don't you ride back with us and lay over at the Three-Bar, and then see what you want to do in the morning?"

Weaver glanced at each of the other two. He looked worried. "I guess so," he said. "I hate to run out on my job, but I don't like to just sit here and wait to get picked off."

That night after supper, Weaver was pretty well sobered up. Back in the bunkhouse he said to Monte and Johnny, "I've got to get out of here. I can feel it."

The other two nodded.

"I already tried to leave this country, but I didn't have enough of a stake. Now I know I've stuck around too long." He took out his tobacco and papers, and as he rolled his cigarette he said, "It takes forever to make a month's wages. If I had somethin' else to sell, I would. All I've got is that little place in the west. If I could sell it, I could be way the hell and gone."

"Where exactly is it?" Johnny asked.

"It's out by Crowheart, out on the other side of Poison Creek and the Badwater."

"Is it in the mountains?" Monte asked.

"Just as you start to get into 'em. Really pretty country, actually. I just couldn't make a go of it on a hundred and sixty acres." Weaver looked at Monte. "It's got a little cabin. Nothin' fancy, but I spent a winter in it."

"What's it worth?" Monte asked.

Weaver lit his cigarette. "It's not worth anything if I can't sell it. So I guess it's worth whatever I can get out of it."

Monte chewed on his toothpick. "Well, I didn't really have it in mind to try to buy any land, but I did want to see those mountains out there, and that would give me a place to hole up."

Weaver held his cigarette between his thumb and first two fingers. "Well, let's give it a try. How much can you offer?"

"I don't have much cash, but let's see what you think of this. I've got that horse I bought from Conde, and I've got a rifle, and I can throw in twenty dollars. I know that's not much, but that's what I've got."

"Well, it's somethin'. Is the horse any good?"

"Oh, yeah. Conde had a pack on it, and then he showed off riding it bareback."

"And the rifle's the one you were carryin' today?"

"Uh-huh. That Winchester."

Weaver thought for a long moment and then said, "I think I'd better take it."

Monte felt a twinge of guilt. "I don't know what else I can offer. I don't have anything else of any real value. I hope I'm helpin' you out."

"Oh, you are. A gun and a horse both travel light, and they're worth something." Weaver paused and then said, "I can write you out a quitclaim deed. You shouldn't have any trouble. Of course, you'd have to finish proving up on it to get a clear title."

Monte said, "I wish I had more to spare."

Weaver said, "No, that's all right." Then he had a sad look on his face as he said, "I appreciate it. I appreciate you stickin' up for me back at camp, too."

"It's all right," Monte said. "Someone had to."

The next morning, Monte and Johnny rode back out with Weaver to his camp. Everything looked the same as it had the evening before. Even the quarter-full whiskey bottle still sat by the fire pit.

"Do you want help doin' anything?" Johnny asked as they dismounted.

"No, thanks," Weaver answered. "I think I can manage. I can roll everything up and pack it on this horse, then get back to Lurie's in good daylight. He won't like it, but I can't help that at this point."

Monte unstrapped his rifle scabbard and handed it, with the rifle inside, toward Weaver.

"Just set it by the tent," said Weaver, who had reins in his left hand and the lead rope to the pack-horse in his right.

Monte set the rifle and scabbard in front of the tent and went back to the other men.

Weaver transferred the lead rope to his left hand to shake hands with Johnny and then Monte.

"So long, boys," said Weaver. "Thanks for your help. I hope to see you again sometime. In the meanwhile, if you can't have fun makin' it, have fun spendin' it."

The boys said "So long," then mounted up, tipped their hats, and rode away. Half a mile out they turned back and waved.

"He looks better today than he did yesterday," Johnny said.

"Yes, he does. But he still looks worried."

Johnny expelled a breath. "With damn good reason, I'd say."

Chapter Seven

The country looked the same as it had the day before. The landscape stretched away in rolls and rumples in all directions. To the north and around to the east, Monte saw a rim of higher ground—hills and bluffs, buttes and mesas. Far to the south lay a pine-covered ridge that ran east and west. In the west rose the mountains, beginning in tree-spotted foothills and then rising in dark, shaggy slopes. In the thin, clear air it was easy to see landmarks for thirty miles or more, and mountains much farther than that. Today the wind was faint, so a rider was more apt to keep his head up and look around.

Monte took in the country on all sides, still and peaceful. If this country changed at all, it did so very slowly. An eight-foot cedar might be a hundred years old, he had heard, and even a fast-growing tree like a cottonwood had a short growing season. Changes in the smaller plant life were even less noticeable.

Changes made by people took a long time to go away, also. On the Oregon Trail he had seen wagon ruts nearly fifty years old. A small circle of rocks for a campfire might stay around, with dirt blowing in over the ashes, long after the men who used it had passed on. Abandoned cabins rotted slowly, and dugouts fell in little by little.

Although the land looked the same as it had the day before, it didn't feel the same. Yesterday the landscape was a broad expanse of dips and rises and occasional watercourses where here and there someone might be changing a brand, or—if that was what Weaver had been doing—changing socks. Today the land was all of that, but it was also a place where at least one man lived in fear, two lived in worry, and three lived in ill will. That wasn't counting Conde, who was probably just hoping to get out before he ran out of tailor-made cigarettes.

Monte and his young pal Johnny rode south after leaving Weaver's camp. They worked the country as before, circling out and meeting up, looking for something out of place amidst the grass and sage and cactus. By now Monte was recognizing cattle he had seen on the earlier rides. He recognized minor landmarks, also, such as an old buffalo wallow or a dry streambed. For the second time he rode past the dried carcass of a cow, its pale ribs showing spots beneath the dark, parched hide. The skeleton was intact, laid out in what was now its proper place. Monte imagined that in the larger order of things, the coyotes had come and chewed, the magpies had pecked and pulled, the flies had laid eggs, and the ants had marched in and out in columns. Now the sun and wind were doing the slower work.

As he and Johnny were eating their cold midday meal, Monte glanced at his horse and remembered that he wasn't carrying a rifle. He asked Johnny if he thought Thane was very particular on that point.

"I don't think it's a big item," Johnny said. "But you might want to get another one."

Monte recalled the evening before, when Weaver had stayed in the bunkhouse. Johnny had told Thane they had run into a couple of Elswick's hands and had had "a little scrape but no shootin'." Monte had sensed at the time that Johnny was helping Weaver save face, which he probably was. Now it occurred to him that Johnny might have the habit of telling Thane only the necessary minimum rather than spilling his guts and going into the last detail, such as the trade between Monte and Weaver.

Monte yawned and was about to make an idle comment when he heard a gunshot in the east. He looked in that direction, and after another moment he heard another shot. "Sounds like a pistol," he said.

"Sure does. What do you say we go take a look?"

"I think so." Monte stood up, brushed off the crumbs, and stuck the last piece of meat in his mouth. He tightened the cinch on his horse and mounted up.

Johnny came up and around on his saddle with his jaw bulged out. "I'll wash the dishes," he said, catching his other stirrup. Then the horses were off in a lope.

They heard a third shot and a fourth, evenly spaced by about a minute. The riders slowed their horses to a fast walk.

"I don't think that's signal shots," said Johnny.

"No, it sounds like target practice. All the same, I think we might want to come up on it slow and easy."

"Uh-huh."

As the horses moved on, Monte took stock of where he was. It was the southern end of the ride, and they were still to the west of the main trail, headed east. The fifth shot sounded close, so he held up his hand and signaled to Johnny. They slowed their horses to a regular walk.

Monte saw a rise off to the left and motioned with his head. Johnny nodded and followed. A sixth shot sounded as they dismounted at the base of the knoll.

Johnny handed his reins to Monte. "I'll go first," he said.

Monte stood with the horses as Johnny walked, bowlegged and leaning forward, up the slope. Toward the top he took off his hat and inched forward. Then he scooted back and came down the hill with his toes forward.

"Go see for yourself," he said, reaching to take the reins.

Monte climbed up the hillside as Johnny had done, leaning forward to keep balance and a low profile, then crawling the last few yards with his hat in his hand. As his eyes crested the hill, he saw a calm scene in front of him less than a hundred yards away.

Elswick sat at three-quarter profile on a dark horse, holding the reins to a brown horse with an empty saddle. Ten yards to the right, wide-hatted and long-haired, stood Pool with a gleaming pistol in his right hand. He had apparently finished reloading it after the first six shots. He held it out at arm's length, raised it, and fired. As a spurt of dust rose from a mound of dirt another seventy yards beyond, Monte saw that Pool was shooting at prairie dogs. The gunman moved his arm to the right, and following the motion, Monte saw a dusty blond figure raised up on its haunches at the mouth of a burrow. Dirt flew up to the left side of the target as the report of the gun came back to the hill where Monte knelt. The prairie dog had vanished.

Monte thought Pool was practicing a ways out of pistol range, until he glanced around and saw, closer in, evidence of Pool's marksmanship. Within about sixty yards of the gunman, three prairie dogs lay dead on the mounds of their separate burrows. Pool had done all right within normal range, and having killed all he was likely to kill there, he had moved out a little farther and was still coming close.

The right arm came up again and moved to the left, then was raised as dirt kicked up in the distance and the sound of the shot crashed in the thin air.

Monte dropped back and moved away, then sidestepped down the hill to rejoin Johnny where he held the horses.

"Our friends," Johnny said in a low voice as another shot went off.

Monte looked up at his own hat brim as he tucked out the corners of his mouth. He took the reins and mounted up softly, as did Johnny. They moved away at a slow walk, hearing another shot and then one more.

When they had gone about half a mile, Monte said, "He's a pretty good shot. I saw where he had killed three out of his first six shots."

Johnny made a clicking sound in the corner of his mouth. "He doesn't need much practice. I bet Elswick buys his ammunition for him, or he wouldn't be wastin' that much." After a moment's silence he added, "Isn't that just like Elswick, though? Workin' on the prairie dog problem, and makin' the range better for all of us."

It had been the first time Monte had seen Elswick since that day in town. He had seen only a partial side view, but it had been enough to bring up a wave of dislike. "Yeah," he said. "A real civic leader."

The boys worked their way back north and then west, toward the ranch. The wind came out of the northwest now, and gray clouds were beginning to pile up.

"If we get a storm, it might push these cattle over east a ways," Johnny said. "But then they'll drift back. I don't think there's much to worry about now, and we might as well get back in good time this evening."

The air was starting to smell like it did when a snowstorm was on its way. As the boys rode into the ranch, Monte sensed a feeling of comfort. The bunkhouse, ranch house, and barn made a safe-looking scene as the wind blew down over the sheltering hills and scattered leaves across the ranch yard. It was this time of year, he thought, when a fellow appreciated a bunkhouse or cabin.

It snowed that night. The next morning showed about two inches of snow on the ground, with a high cloud cover. The wind was gusting off and on, now from the north and now from the west. The horses were frisky but caused no trouble as the boys got saddled and mounted for the morning ride.

They rode east again. A new snow would make it easy to read any of the day's activities, including their own. Monte saw nothing for the first mile out; then he saw a coyote about a quarter mile away, its long tail streaming behind it as it went up and over a rise. It was a common sight, coyotes out hunting after a snowstorm, and the world seemed in order.

By midmorning the wind had gentled down but the snow had not melted. The boys had seen jackrabbit tracks, coyote tracks, cattle tracks, and their own as they circled around. The snow had given more to read, but otherwise the ride had been routine.

"I'll tell you what," Johnny said as they rested the horses. "We're not too far from Weaver's camp. We ought to ride on over there and see if he got away all right."

"Wouldn't hurt," Monte said.

They rode straight to the north then, with a cold breeze in their faces. Monte was glad he hadn't shaved since Sunday; even that much stubble made his face feel protected.

They found the little creek, which had a blanket of snow except in the very center where the water trickled. They followed it downstream, and when they passed the grove of box elders, Monte was surprised to see the white tent still in place. He hadn't seen it sooner because of the white background and the screen of trees.

He looked at Johnny, who looked back with a warning frown and said nothing.

Beyond the tent, both horses grazed at the ends of their picket ropes. Neither horse had anything on its back. The scene was silent and motionless, even as Monte moved his gaze in closer and saw Weaver sitting by the fire pit.

The riders moved closer, their horses making soft thuds on the ground. They dismounted at about a hundred feet out, and getting no answer to their call, they walked on in. Monte could see Weaver's hat pushed forward, almost meeting with the bushy blond mustache. The hat brim had snow on it, as did Weaver's overcoat and the saddle he leaned against.

Monte and Johnny stopped a few feet from the body. Johnny leaned over and picked up the whiskey bottle, which, with the snow shaken off, proved to be empty.

Johnny looked at Monte. "Must have had too much of this and fell asleep. Froze to death." He dropped the bottle on the ground.

Monte grimaced. "Not unless he had another bottle of it. It wouldn't have lasted him that long." He

113

looked out at the horses, back at the tent, and again at Weaver. "It looks to me like he put his horses out for a little bit, then sat down to think it all over before he packed up his camp."

"We can see," Johnny said. He handed his reins to Monte and squatted at Weaver's side. He opened the coat and closed it back up, then looked upward at Monte. "He's been shot, all right. Square in the chest."

Monte shook his head. "You could think that he waited too long, but he wouldn't have been sittin' here all that long anyway. They just waited until we were gone a ways. And if they hadn't gotten him here, they would've gotten him while he was rollin' up his tent, or whatever. Maybe they did, but with this snow on top of everything, it would be hard to tell." He thought for a second. "He ought to have two rifles, and I don't see any here."

He went to the tent, untied the flap, and peeked in. He saw a canvas duffel bag, a tossed heap of bedclothes, and a slicker with a few food provisions wrapped in cotton bags sitting on it.

"Both rifles are gone," he said as he walked back to Johnny. He looked out at the horses on their pickets. "It's a wonder they didn't take the horses, but I guess they're harder to hide and easier to identify." Monte looked at the sorrel horse and remembered Conde's cheerful comment that it would carry out anything as long as it was dead. He doubted that Conde had had a hand in this piece of work.

"That's some people for you," Johnny said.

"They'll kill a man but don't want to be called a horse thief."

Monte looked down at Weaver. This was a rotten move. Sure, Weaver had gotten drunk and spouted off, but that was no reason to gun him down. They didn't give him a chance. They wouldn't have. However they did it, they had to have propped him up. Then they put his bottle next to him, just to mock him in the end. They might have even poured out the whiskey.

Monte felt his throat tightening as he looked at the man he had tried to help. It had come to nothing, but he was glad he had done it. Weaver had done something stupid, had realized it, and had tried to make up for it by getting away, even if it meant losing face. But they didn't give him a chance.

Monte swallowed and looked at Johnny. "Pool and Elswick were way the hell over south, weren't they?"

"They sure were."

"Handy, huh? Makin' a lot of noise. They could've set that up. But that doesn't mean they couldn't have come by here. They had all morning."

Johnny picked at his mustache. "Yep, they did. And like he said, where the hell's the law when you need it?" He twisted his mouth and then said, "I suppose we'd better go tell Lurie."

The Three-Bar riders approached Lurie's place from the south. On the left side of the layout was a long, low building that looked like the bunkhouse. Beyond that, still on the left, sat a large two-story

115

house with a porch on the east side. Across from the house was a tall barn with hayloft doors. Connected to it, a stable ran parallel to the bunkhouse. A large pole corral reached out behind the barn and stable.

Johnny got down from his horse and ducked into the bunkhouse just long enough for the door to close and open again. He came out walking fast and closing the door behind him.

"In the big house," he said, swinging back onto his horse.

They rode forward another forty yards. Johnny looked at Monte as if to say it was his turn. Monte dismounted and handed his reins to Johnny.

He took a deep breath as he walked up the wooden steps. Hearing no footsteps, he knocked on the solid wood door. He knocked again. Then the door opened, and he stood face-to-face with Dora.

An apprehensive look crossed her face right away. "Why did you come here?" she asked.

"Don't worry. It's not about you. I came to talk to your husband. It's about one of his men."

Her face relaxed, and for a second she looked pretty with her golden hair, blue eyes, and fair skin. "I'm sorry," she said. "If you don't mind waiting a minute, I'll go get him."

"That's fine."

She closed the door until it touched the jamb but did not latch. As he heard her footsteps go away, he turned around to look at Johnny and exchange nods.

At least two minutes had passed when he heard footsteps, heavier this time. The door opened to reveal Carson Lurie in his vest and shirtsleeves.

He looked at Monte and beyond him, in the direction of Johnny. "You're Thane's man, aren't you?"

"Yes, I am." Monte glanced beyond Lurie into the vestibule and saw nothing; he wondered what the little girl looked like and whether he would ever see her.

"Well, what is it?" Lurie gave him a sharp look with his blue eyes.

"It's your man Weaver. He ran into some trouble."

Lurie's face tightened. "What kind of trouble?"

"With Elswick's men. Johnny and I were at his camp the day before yesterday, when Thrall and another fella came in. Thrall started a fight, but it didn't go very far. Weaver went back with us to spend the night at the Three-Bar, and the next morning we went back out there with him. Then, when we went to check on him this morning, he was dead. Looks like it happened yesterday. It snowed since then, so it's hard to see any sign."

"You left him there by himself? Why didn't someone come and tell me there was trouble?"

Monte was irked that Lurie would blame him for leaving Weaver alone, when Lurie himself had put him out there for over a week. Monte brushed his irritation aside. "He said he was coming back himself. He told us he didn't need any help, so we left. But they didn't even let him get out of camp."

Lurie had his jaw set sideways. "Who's 'they'?"

"I don't know. Whoever came for him after we

117

left. It happened sometime yesterday before the snow, like I said."

Lurie's face, having paled somewhat, looked pasty. "I don't like the sound of this at all." His glance went out beyond Monte and then came back. "Wait here if you would—or with your partner there. I'll be out in a few minutes."

Monte walked down the steps and into the yard. He took the reins from Johnny, who had dismounted. They stood without saying anything for a few minutes until Lurie came out of the house carrying his coat and putting on his hat.

"Let's go see Farrell," he said.

They walked across to the barn, where Lurie called out Farrell's name as he put on his coat.

In a moment, Farrell pushed open the big door and came out. His sleeves were rolled up and his hands were bloody. He held a bloody knife in his right hand. Monte assumed he had been butchering an animal.

"Weaver's been killed," Lurie said. "I need you to go out with these boys and bring him in."

Monte looked at Johnny, who gave a short nod.

Farrell's face showed no expression as he looked at his boss and said, "I suppose I should bring along a packhorse for his camp."

Lurie took a deep breath and exhaled. "I guess so." He looked at the other two men. "Is the saddle horse still there?"

Monte answered. "Actually, he's got two horses there. His saddle horse and another one."

Farrell's question came out sharp. "Where'd he get the other one?"

"He got it from me," Monte answered. "He knew he was in trouble, and he wanted to pack his traps and get out." Monte looked at Lurie. "So whatever becomes of his personal effects, that sorrel horse is his."

"For as much good as it did him," Lurie said. He looked at Farrell. "Well, go ahead."

Monte and Johnny didn't get back to the Three-Bar until after dark. Thane and Horace were sitting at the table beneath a tobacco haze when the boys came in from putting the horses away. Thane asked what the trouble was, so Johnny gave him the full story. He started by retelling the incident of the fight, this time in more detail, and finished by saying they had gotten Weaver and his belongings back to Lurie's ranch.

"Well, it was good of you to help," Thane said as he set his pipe aside.

Monte spoke up. "I don't know, but I think I might have made things worse."

Thane shook his head. "This was a move against Lurie from the start. Weaver got caught in the middle of it. Elswick sent Thrall in there to pick a fight. That's evident. From the sounds of it, things worked out just the way Elswick would have liked, although Thrall might disagree on a couple of points." Thane shook his head again. "It's too bad about Weaver. But don't blame yourself. You stuck up for him and you tried to help him get out. It just wasn't enough."

"Well, where does that leave us?" Johnny asked.

"Next in line, maybe," said Thane. He used his

right forefinger to smooth the beard on his chin as he gazed at the ceiling. "I need to send a wire to the sheriff to find out when he's coming back." He brought his glance back to the table. "Go ahead and get cleaned up, boys, and eat supper. I'll have the two of you ride into town tomorrow to send the wire for me. How does that sound?"

"Fine with me," said Johnny.

"Me, too," Monte added. He had an image of dark hair and a bright smile. Then he thought of Weaver, wrapped in canvas and laid out in a wagon bed in the Circle-L barn. He remembered the last words he had heard Weaver say. *If you can't have fun makin' it, have fun spendin' it.* November had thirty days, so he had made exactly one dollar today. Tomorrow had to be better.

Chapter Eight

It made sense for Thane to send his two riders on the errand. With a man just having been killed, Thane would not be wise to make the trip by himself; and if he was going to occupy one of his men for that purpose, he could just as well send the two of them out as usual. Besides, there was nothing that Thane had to do personally. He wrote out the message, folded it in a second piece of paper, and gave it to Johnny Romaine, who was to deliver it and then wait around town until a response came back. Monte thought the plan was reasonable, especially since it also allowed a stretch of time for him and Johnny to be on their own.

In the morning, Monte was not surprised to see Johnny wearing the horsehair watch chain. He himself had put the ivory token, in its cloth wrapping, in his coat pocket. Both he and Johnny had cleaned and shaved, and even though a man had been found shot dead the day before, a tone of optimism hung in the bunkhouse.

"Don't come back wearin' too much perfume," said Horace as they all drank a cup of coffee after breakfast.

Thane was tamping his pipe in a second attempt to light it. "The perfume isn't so bad," he said, studying his work. "But be careful with the lice. It's been a year since we had any of them, and Horace doesn't like you to use up all his kerosene dousing yourself."

"Well, I'll stay away from the Indians and the nesters." Johnny swayed his head as he lowered it to take a sip of his coffee.

Thane struck a match and waited for it to build a flame. "If they were the only ones we had to worry about, we wouldn't have said a thing." He gave Monte a sly look. "Isn't that right?"

"So I've heard."

The cheerful conversation went on. Thane said that if the snow melted off by dinnertime, he and Horace might go out for a while and look for arrowheads.

"Have you found quite a few?" asked Monte.

"Horace has a good collection," Thane answered. Monte looked at Horace, who nodded.

"We won't go too far out," Thane added, "so don't worry about us."

Monte doubted that there was much to worry about. He was sure both men could take care of themselves well enough. They probably wanted to get out and look around, just for the peace of mind it would bring. It would also keep away cabin fever, and it might add to Horace's collection.

The ride into town went without incident. Monte and his partner Johnny saw cattle from time to time and detoured to look at them, but nothing seemed out of the ordinary. On any ride they were likely to see at least a half-dozen brands, as they did today. Cattle with one brand mixed with those of another, red and brown and brindle. They showed no recognition of ownership; Three-Bar cattle and Circle L cattle ran alike from any horse and rider. The cattle moved over the open range with no regard for boundaries except natural obstacles such as a bluff or canyon. Cattle obviously didn't care who owned them or who, if anybody, owned the land.

That was why cattle were owned and people were owners, Monte thought. Men had a sense of property. Monte had understood that, even though he had never had more than his own personal things. It made sense to protect property and the things a man had worked for. He could even understand why some men would want to take the property of others. But he had a harder time understanding why men were willing to kill others, or pay to have them killed, for the sake of extending property. And yet that seemed to be why Elswick brought in Pool and why, two or three moves later, Weaver had been killed. Weaver had made some strong comments, but he would not even have done that if Thrall had not come to pick a fight on Elswick's behalf. For a few hundred head of drooling beasts and the chance to control the land they wandered over, a man was willing to send out another man alone; and a third man, whoever he was, was willing to send a bullet through the second man's chest.

Monte spoke up, to pull himself out of the dreary thoughts. "Where does Horace find his arrowheads?"

"Oh, just about anywhere. I think he finds more of 'em in the spring, but now's a good time, too." Johnny looked at the sky. "Looks like they might be able to get out and do some lookin' around today."

Johnny continued in good spirits. After he and Monte saw to it that the telegram went out, he took leave of Monte as before. A tacit agreement existed between them: Johnny had a visit to make, and Monte was easy to find.

The café smelled of breakfast food, coffee, and tobacco smoke as Monte stepped inside. Two men who looked like merchants were sitting at the middle table on the right. They looked up, noted him, and went back to their conversation. Ramona came out of the kitchen, drying her hands on her apron. Her face brightened, and she raised her right hand to brush her hair back from her right cheek. She remained standing by the left table in the back, so Monte went to that table.

He took off his hat. "Good morning."

"Good morning. Have you had breakfast?"

"I sure did. Before we left."

"You'd like some coffee, then?"

"Please." He took off his coat and sat down facing the door as she walked away.

When she came back with the coffeepot and the cup, she said, "We got a little snow here."

"We did, too. A couple of inches."

She poured the coffee and straightened up. "Have you been busy?"

He imagined from her question that Lurie might not have come to town yet, or if he had, the full story had not yet circulated. "Busy enough," he said. Then, catching a curious look and remembering the other two men in the café, he said, "Boss sends us out on a ride every day. Today he sent us into town to send a telegram."

"Oh." She gave an affirmative nod and moved away.

He watched her as she walked to the other table and poured coffee. He liked her movements; they were part of her presence, which he found charming. She did not stay long at the other table, and the two men barely glanced up from their conversation.

She came back to stand by his table. She placed herself at his left, facing the restaurant. "How is your horse?" she asked.

He felt a radiance in her closeness, and the question took him by surprise. In his own mind, the purchase of the horse had faded into the past, shadowed by larger events.

"Oh," he said, "I don't have that horse anymore. I traded it." Then, realizing he had just created another question, he added, "I traded it, along with a couple of other things—a rifle and some money— for a cabin."

"A cabin? Really? Near the ranch where you work?"

"No, it's quite a ways from here. It's off in the

125

west, out toward the mountains that I told you I wanted to go see."

"Oh. Then you'll have a place to stay."

He sipped his coffee. "That was my idea, I guess."

Her hands were together now. Her right thumb was rubbing the backs of her left fingers. "Are you going to go pretty soon, then?"

He gave her the best smile he could, and he felt his eyes relax. "I'm still not in any hurry."

"Well, that's good." She glanced at the other two men and back at him. "If you'll excuse me, I need to go into the kitchen and do some work. I'll be back out in a little while."

Monte sat and sipped on his coffee. After another ten minutes, the two men got up from their table. Ramona came out from the kitchen and tended to them, and they left. She put the money in the pocket of her apron and came back to stand by Monte's table.

"Those men were talking about a man who got killed. I heard a little bit of it before you came in."

Monte looked straight at her. "Was it a man who worked for Lurie?"

"Yes. Then you heard of it, too."

Monte lowered his voice. "More than that. Johnny and I found him." He glanced around, even though he knew there was no one else in the café. "It was the fellow I traded the horse to, as it turns out. He had a run-in with one of Elswick's men, and not long after that we found him dead."

"Then this happened out by your ranch?"

"Well, yes. Out on the range between Thane, Lurie, and Elswick's places. It's open country, so everyone's cattle graze out there."

Her face had a drawn look. "That's not good at all, to have someone killed."

"No, not at all. They just shot him and left him there. Took his rifle and the one he got from me."

"Then you don't have a rifle anymore?"

"Not at the moment. But I might have to get one."

She laid her hand on his arm. "You're not going to get into the fight, are you?"

The hand on his arm felt gentle, although it stayed for only a few seconds. "I'm trying to stay out of trouble," he said, "but I had a run-in with that one fellow myself."

"Which one?"

"His name is Thrall."

"Euh," she said with a shudder. "He makes me sick."

"I imagine he comes in here, then."

"Oh, yes. I don't like the way he watches me."

Monte glanced at the door again. "I don't like anything about him."

"Oh, he smells. And he says such . . . vulgar things."

Monte felt a tenseness coming to him. "Oh?"

"Yes. He made a proposition. He asked me to go with him. For money."

Monte felt his stomach tighten. He imagined Thrall would take that sort of liberty because Ramona was a working woman and was no longer married—something like the saying about no harm taking a slice off a cut loaf. Maybe her skin color had something to do with it, too. Men didn't treat decent women that way and get away with it—not out here, where women were so scarce. The way men saw it, there were two kinds of women—the decent ones, that a man didn't say a cross word about or even mention in some places, and the other ones, that a man could address with language appropriate to those places. Thrall should know the difference as well as anyone, so he had evidently made some coarse assumptions about Ramona.

Monte looked at her. "Did he say that in here?"

"Yes," she answered. "And I told him he wasn't welcome to come in here anymore. But I see him out on the street, and I have the feeling that he still watches me."

She had a pained look on her face, and Monte had a feeling of revulsion to match.

She glanced at the door. "Do you think he had anything to do with, you know, the man who worked for Mr. Lurie?"

"Indirectly, maybe, insofar as he had a squabble with Weaver—that was the fellow's name, by the way. But we don't know who really did the killing. My guess is that Elswick had another man do it." He lowered his voice even more. "Do you know a fellow that goes by the name of Pool?"

"The longhair?"

"That's him."

"Yes, I know him. He came in here once with the other one, but he didn't say anything."

"That's just as well."

"I say so. He gives me the shivers."

A minute passed without either of them speaking. Finally Monte thought of something to say.

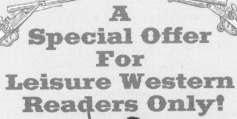

GET YOUR 4 FREE* BOOKS NOW— A VALUE BETWEEN $16 AND $20

Mail the Free* Book Certificate Today!

FREE* BOOKS CERTIFICATE!

YES! I want to subscribe to the Leisure Western Book Club. Please send me my 4 FREE* BOOKS. Then, each month, I'll receive the four newest Leisure Western Selections to preview FREE* for 10 days. If I decide to keep them, I will pay the Special Member's Only discounted price of just $3.36 each, a total of $13.44 ($14.50 US in Canada). This saves me between $3 and $6 off the bookstore price. There are no shipping, handling or other charges.* There is no minimum number of books I must buy and I may cancel the program at any time. In any case, the 4 FREE* BOOKS are mine to keep—at a value of between $17 and $20!

*In Canada, add $5.00 Canadian shipping and handling per order for first shipment. For all subsequent shipments to Canada the cost of membership in the Book Club is $14.50 US, which includes $7.50 shipping and handling per month. All payments must be made in US currency.

Name _____

Address _____

City_____ State_____ Country_____

Zip_____Telephone_____

Tear here and mail your FREE* book card today!

Get Four Books Totally
F R E E* —
A Value between
$16 and $20

Tear here and mail your FREE* book card today!

PLEASE RUSH
MY FOUR FREE*
BOOKS TO ME
RIGHT AWAY!

LeisureWestern Book Club
P.O. Box 6613
Edison, NJ 08818-6613

AFFIX
STAMP
HERE

"How about your own horse? How is he?"

Her face was relaxed again. "Oh, just fine. I thought we could go over and look at him, as soon as I finish some things in the kitchen."

"Go ahead," he said. "I can wait."

In a few minutes she was ready to go, so Monte put on his hat and coat and walked her to the door. "You leave the place unlocked, as I recall."

"Uh-huh."

He gave her his arm to help her step down from the sidewalk. Once in the street, she put her hands into her coat pockets. He liked the feeling of having her by his side as they crossed the street and walked toward the livery stable.

Movement in the sky caught his eye. Looking up, he saw a flock of wild geese in a V formation headed north. He could barely hear the swish of their wings. Ramona looked up also; then she and Monte looked at each other and smiled.

At the stable, Monte found a halter, comb, and brush while Ramona spoke a few words to the stable keeper. Monte went to the pen and brought the bay horse inside.

The horse was easy to work with once again. Monte tied him in the stall, brushed him down, and resumed the task of combing out the dark mane. He worked with small strands, pulling the steel comb through the tangles. From time to time he looked across at Ramona, who smiled back each time.

When he had the mane combed out all the way, he walked away from the horse for a moment. "I suppose you need to get back to your work," he

John D. Nesbitt

said. "I'm not anxious for you to leave, but I don't want to keep you away from it." He pointed with the comb. "I can do some work on the tail. It'll take some time, but I think I've got plenty. We don't have to go back until we get an answer to the telegram."

She moved to the gate and put her hands on it. "I don't like to just leave you here doing my work."

"It's all right," he said, patting her right hand with his left and then withdrawing it. She didn't move her hand, so he felt encouraged to say more. "But before you go, I had something I thought I'd like to mention."

Her eyes tensed for a second and then relaxed. "Go ahead."

He fidgeted with the comb between both hands, then kept it in his right as he put his left hand into his coat pocket. "I have a little somethin' I wanted to show you. It's not much, but it struck my fancy when I first saw it." He brought out the small bundle. "I don't know if you'll care for it, but I wanted to show it to you."

He unwrapped the cloth and held it with the ivory token in his open palm. It looked elegant, with the dark etching against the pale ivory.

She took a small, short breath. "It's beautiful."

"I'm glad you like it." Their eyes met, and he went on. "I don't know if you'd like to have it, but if you would, I'd like to give it to you."

"You mean, as a gift?"

"Yes, exactly that. I bought it quite a while back, and I thought maybe someday I'd meet someone I'd like to give it to. If you think you can accept it, I'd like you to have it. Just as a gift."

130

Her eyes were moist and full of expression as they met his again. "Thank you," she said. "It's very pretty."

Still she did not touch it, and he was afraid she was going to speak another sentence beginning with the word "but." He moved his hand an inch forward, and she took the piece of ivory in her right hand. She rubbed her thumb lightly across the surface.

"Thank you," she said again.

"You're welcome, Ramona." He liked the sound of her name as he spoke it. He wanted more than anything to kiss her—on the forehead, on the cheek, on the lips—but he feared he would ruin the moment. "Take the cloth, too," he said.

She lifted the cloth with her left hand and laid the piece of ivory on it in her palm. Then she folded the cloth and put the small bundle in her left coat pocket.

He put his right hand on top of the gate, and she laid her right hand gently upon it. He touched the back of her hand with his left as he pressed with his right.

She drew back and looked down; when she looked up, he thought he saw a faint blush on her face. "I should go," she said. "I've been gone for quite a while."

"Go ahead. I'll work at this a little longer, and then I'll come see you."

"That would be fine."

She had her mouth drawn together in an almost serious expression, which he interpreted as shyness. He felt elated, with his nervousness all gone, so he winked. She smiled, then turned and walked away.

He felt happy now as he stood by the hindquarter of the horse and pulled the tail around to work on it. His tension had lifted. A pretty girl—not just any pretty girl, but Ramona—had accepted his gift. She had seemed a little hesitant, but she had smiled at the last moment. Things couldn't have gone any better.

When he had the horse's tail combed out, he took a look at the hooves, picking up each one and looking at the underside. He gave the horse another brushing and then turned him out in the pen with the others.

Back out on the street, he looked up in the sky to see if any more geese were flying. There were none, but this was the time of year to see them. Some of them headed farther south, he knew, for he had seen them in Colorado and New Mexico. But many of them wintered in this part of the country. He knew that farmers were beginning to settle in, especially to the south and east; that would provide feed in addition to the native grass seeds. And there was water, too, with the various little creeks and then the river to the north and east. The geese they had seen flying north had probably eaten in one place and were going to find water in another.

The café was empty again when he went in. Smelling fried beef and fresh coffee, he realized it was getting close to dinnertime. As he walked back to the table where he had been sitting earlier, Ramona came out of the kitchen. He thought she had an air of mild embarrassment about her, or shyness at least.

"I forgot to pay for my coffee," he said.

"Oh, no," she said, brightening up and waving her finger. "Not today. Not after all the work you've done for me."

"It wasn't much."

"That doesn't matter. It's a lot to me."

He took off his coat and sat down. "Well, all right."

"Dinner will be ready in a little while," she said. "And I want you to accept it, like the coffee."

He squirmed. "I don't know if I'd feel right. I'd feel like I was mooching."

Her confidence seemed to be coming back, here in her own place. Her eyes sparkled as she said, "You don't want to hurt my feelings, do you?"

He put up his hands. "Oh, no. Not at all."

"Then you will eat. And you will drink coffee."

He grinned. "All right."

When she came back with the coffee she asked, "Where is that place where you said you're going?"

He looked up at her. "Well, I didn't say for sure I was going there, but I hope to. The place where I bought the cabin, as I understand it, is called Crowheart. That's the nearest place-name. He wrote out directions along with the bill of sale and all."

"Crowheart. That's a pretty name, isn't it?"

"I guess so."

She went back into the kitchen, and in a little while she brought him a plate of fried beefsteak and potatoes. She set it down in front of him, then went away and came back with a tin plate of biscuits.

She paused as if she was going to say something, so he held off with his knife and fork.

"I want to tell you again, before other people come in, that I appreciate the gift. Thank you."

The tenderness in her voice brought moisture to his eyes. "You're welcome. I was hoping that this way, you would have roses in the winter."

Her eyes were shining as she said, "I will. They're very pretty."

He laid his left hand, palm up, on the edge of the table near her. She reached with her right hand and touched her fingertips to his, then drew back her hand. The silence between them was better than words.

Chapter Nine

The next morning, as the tobacco haze formed after breakfast, Thane summarized the message that Johnny had conveyed to him. The sheriff was making progress with his treatment but needed some time to regain his strength before traveling back to Eagle Spring.

"So it looks as if we're still on our own for a while," he said, raising his eyebrows and looking around at Horace and the two hired hands. "We need to be out and about and keep our eyes open, but we don't want to do anything careless or start any trouble. And we don't want to worry ourselves into the ground. I'm not afraid to ride to Lurie's by myself, but if we go anywhere east, including to town, we had better go two together."

He look around the table, and the others nodded. Monte spoke up. "Lurie's not going to send out

Farrell by himself, is he?" He doubted that Lurie would ride out and work the range himself.

Thane's hazel eyes widened. "I hope not. Anybody can see now that it was a mistake to send out Weaver like he did. By the way, is there going to be a burial for Weaver?"

Johnny answered. "Lurie's gonna have the body shipped back to Iowa, to his kinfolks."

Thane nodded. "Well, that's one thing I want to talk to Lurie about—Farrell, that is, and how Lurie wants to use him. I don't know if he wants to hire someone else or if he might want to go together on this and have Farrell work with you boys."

"Seems like we'd cover less ground," Johnny suggested.

"It's a lot of country any way you look at it," Thane answered. "We can't be everywhere at once, but we need to let someone know that we're not letting him ride roughshod over us."

Through conversations with Johnny, Monte had gathered that Thane didn't mind getting out and doing ranch work. Unlike Lurie, he worked as a regular rider during roundup and shipping, except that he didn't night-herd. The rest of the year, he left the routine work to his men as he worked on the business angles of record-keeping and reading up on cattle production. He had things to keep him busy, and moreover, in the present circumstances, he probably didn't want to put himself out as a target.

"So I'm going to ride up to Lurie's in a little while and have a talk with him. You boys can take a ride south and look over that country. Same as always."

All four men got up. Thane put on his coat, picked up his pipe with his left hand, settled his right hand upon the pinched white crown of his hat where it hung on the nail, and then paused as he settled the hat on his head.

"Horace, do you need anything done?"

Horace stopped at the end of the table by the dishpan. He turned down his mouth and shook his head. "No, not really. Nothin' that needs to be done today."

"Well, all right, then." Thane opened the door and went out.

The boys put on their hats and coats and stepped outside. Monte felt the chill right away and put on his gloves. Johnny had his hands in his coat pockets, and after a few steps he put on his gloves, too.

They roped out and saddled their two horses for the day's work, then let the horses stand for a few minutes as they warmed the bits under their coats. After putting on the bridles, they led the horses out of the barn and into the cold morning, where the sounds of boots and spurs and horse hooves rang clear on the hard ground. Most of the snow was gone, except on the north side of the barn where it had been in shade the afternoon before.

The cookhouse door opened, and Horace's voice came across the yard. "Don't forget this." He held up a cloth bag that bulged with the promise of lunch.

The boys crossed the yard. "Thanks, Horace," said Johnny as he took the bag.

Monte thanked him also, and then the two riders mounted up and headed out south.

They did not speak much as they rode. The sun had come up but was not warming things very fast, so the riders were hunched into their coats. For Monte, the day hadn't defined itself very clearly yet. He had good feelings carried over from the day before, and he recalled several moments in which there had been no distance between him and Ramona. But he also had a feeling of worry.

He was visited by images of Weaver that he could not dispel. He kept seeing Weaver drunk and defiant by his fire, dead and slumped by the cold fire pit, laid out and wrapped in a canvas sheet in a wagon bed in Lurie's barn. Weaver was going out of the country now, with not much of a good-bye. Monte imagined he hadn't had many friends out by Crowheart, from the way he talked, and he hadn't been here long enough to make any. All he had done was prime someone's powder and then stand in the way of fire. Even if he had brought some of it on himself, it was unfair. A man was supposed to have more of a chance. And the others, Monte thought, ought to be able to do more about it.

The boys rode on together for quite a ways, seeing cattle now and then. At one point they flushed an antelope doe and her half-grown fawn. The two animals streaked to the west, cut south, and then wheeled west again, yellow-and-white gleams in the morning sunlight. Small as it was, the incident seemed to break the silence.

"A little farther on," Johnny said, "and we get into some bad cactus country." He turned in the saddle and made a circle with his gloved right thumb and forefinger. "Little bitty cactus about this big, with needles an inch long. Are you familiar with it?"

"Some. It's the kind that jumps up and grabs your pants if you're walkin' along on foot. Like little balls."

"That's them. They just hang on the hide of cattle—or deer and antelope, too, for that matter. Sometimes they dig in, though. If we see any of that, we'll do some doctorin'."

After they had split up and rejoined a couple of times, Johnny said he had found a steer that needed some help. It had a lump on its neck. He led the way as he and Monte untied their ropes. About a quarter of a mile to the east, Johnny turned and spoke.

"That's him. He's one of ours."

It was a Durham steer, a two-year-old by the looks of him, with horns long enough to get a rope onto. Monte's horse was onto the steer right away, following the animal on the left as it dodged one way and another. Monte shook out a loop, swung his rope three times, and made his throw. Catching both horns, he pulled the rope to tighten it, then dallied it around the saddle horn as his horse kept pace with the dancing steer.

Johnny, who had been hazing on the right, was swinging his rope now. He flung the rope down and jerked back up with his right hand. His horse settled back as the rope went tight. By the time Monte's horse had moved around to face the steer head-on, Johnny had taken his dallies. The steer hit the ground and raised a small cloud of dust.

"I'll do it," Johnny called out as he came down off the left side of his horse.

The steer had fallen on its right side, so Johnny stepped across his rope at the low end and moved along the spine of the animal, out of the way of the kicking front legs.

Monte kept his horse tight and watched as Johnny reached down to the lump beneath the steer's jaw. The steer flailed and bellowed as Johnny leaned and then jumped back, shaking his gloved hand to dislodge the cactus.

"Got it," he called. He jumped back over the rope, moved quickly to his horse, and climbed aboard.

As the men nudged their horses forward to loosen the ropes, the steer got up onto its feet. Monte and then Johnny shook their ropes loose, and the steer trotted away, shaking its head. Johnny gave a smile with his teeth clenched as he and Monte coiled their ropes.

"That was an easy one," he said.

Half an hour later, as they were riding together, Monte saw a calf with a cactus lodged in its right eyelid. It was a stocky fall calf, a Circle-L Hereford, trotting next to its mother.

"There's one," Monte said.

"And that's his mama," Johnny called back. "Which one do you want?"

"I guess it's my turn. I'll take the calf."

Both men took down their ropes again as Johnny rode between the cow and the calf. Monte's horse picked out the calf and went after it.

The calf bolted as Monte shook out his loop. He spurred the horse and swung his rope, and the horse gave a burst of speed. When he was within twenty-five feet of the calf's head and a little to the left, he made his toss. As he saw the loop settle in front of the pink nose of the white-faced calf, he pulled. He took his dallies fast, then sat back on his stirrups and pulled his reins as the horse settled on its haunches and jerked the calf off its feet.

Monte hit the ground and followed the rope to the calf. The horse was backing up slowly, dragging the calf so it couldn't get back up, while the calf was bawling and kicking up dust. Monte held the rope with his right gloved hand; with his left he reached for the calf's thrashing head. He settled the heel of his hand on the embedded cactus, then brought his fingertips back and gave a yank.

The calf let out a deep-throated bellow, but the cactus came out, attached to Monte's glove. Now he heard Johnny shouting. He turned and saw the back of Johnny and his horse in a cloud of dust, not fifty yards away. The pair was faced off with the mama cow, which was dodging to one side and another in an attempt to get to her calf. The horse was stutter-stepping, and Johnny was hollering at the cow.

Monte ran back up the rope and bailed onto the saddle, then nudged the horse forward. He didn't want that cow to hit the rope. The calf came to its feet as the cow broke around Johnny's right side. Johnny and the horse came pounding after the cow and pushed it away. Monte shook his rope once, twice, three times, and finally a fourth until it loosened on the calf's neck. He flipped the rope forward, and the calf was free.

By now the cow had turned around and was heading back. "Let 'er go," Monte hollered as he hauled in his rope. He realized he still had the cactus in his glove, so he knocked it loose with a tight loop of the rope and then finished coiling.

Johnny came riding over with his horse going at a fast walk. "Some fun, huh?"

"Just barely."

"Well, I'd say Lurie owes us for that little favor."

Monte looked at the heel of his glove and then at the cow and calf, which were trotting away. "I guess," he said. "We'll see who collects."

The rest of the day went without event. The wind picked up in the late morning and blew all through the afternoon. It died down at dusk when the boys were putting the horses away, but then at suppertime it started howling again.

The next morning, the wind was still blowing, so no one was in a hurry after breakfast. Thane and Johnny brought out their smoking materials as usual.

"I wanted to send these boys out after some deer meat," Horace said. "But this weather's no good for it."

The flame went up and down on Thane's match as he drew on his pipe. He exhaled a cloud of smoke, then shook out the match. "That's all right. When the wind settles down, we'll send 'em out."

The wind blew all that day and the next. Thane said there was nothing so urgent that the boys should have to ride out in that sort of weather to check on the range. He put them to work cleaning out the barn and greasing the axles on the two wagons. Mealtimes were long and workdays were short, but Thane made sure they had some work to do.

Monte imagined Elswick's men were probably staying close to home, too. He wondered if Pool did much of anything other than oil his six-gun and sharpen his jack knife.

The wind had let up by Sunday morning, so Johnny and Monte decided they would use part of their day off to make a visit to town. They cleaned up and got decked out as usual. Monte decided to ride his buckskin horse, as it had not had any exercise for a couple of weeks. Johnny said it would be a good time to ride his horse, too, so he roped it out of the corral. Johnny's was a white horse with a few flecks of black.

They had a light wind in their face, brisk but not strong, as they rode into town. They kept an eye on the country, detoured a couple of times to look at cattle, and arrived in town at about midday. Johnny took leave at the first left turn, as he had done on the earlier occasion just a week before.

Monte rode down the main street, noticing a few horses and wagons standing idle. It looked as if the lull in the wind had brought in a few people. Before he had noticed much in detail, the door of the general mercantile store opened, and a man stepped out carrying a fifty-pound bag of flour.

Monte recognized the man as Farrell. His denim trousers reached out beneath the flour sack, and his denim coat squared out above it. His light-colored hat sat back on his head and let the daylight fall upon his face, showing its freckles and light complexion. His washed-out blue eyes glanced in Monte's direction, but no expression crossed his face.

Lurie was standing in back of Farrell, still holding the door open. Monte saw his heavy form, bulked out with the brown wool overcoat, standing to one side. Monte expected to see the storekeeper come out next with a side of bacon or a sack of beans, but he was surprised.

A flash of golden hair told him it was Dora. She was wearing a dark blue overcoat and a matching hat that had her pretty well wrapped up, but her pale face and bright hair were unmistakable. She seemed to hesitate in the doorway as she looked downward; then a little girl stepped out into the daylight.

For a moment, Monte lost sense of everything else as he gazed at the girl. She was about five or six years old, big enough to be her own person but small enough to look like a little angel. She wore a gray hat and coat; in between the gray patches, golden hair like her mother's surrounded her white cheeks and fell on her shoulders.

Dora moved the little girl to the edge of the sidewalk. "Come on, Claire," she said. "Put on your mittens." Dora glanced up at Monte and then away.

By now Monte was passing the wagon where Farrell was stowing the bag of flour. Farrell did not look at him.

Monte rode another thirty yards and turned his horse in to the hitching rail in front of the café. He looked back and saw Dora standing by the front wheel as Carson Lurie lifted the little girl into the wagon. Claire. She seemed to float like an angel.

For as much as it seemed like an illusion, it struck him as the most real detail he had known about Dora since he had come to Eagle Spring. He had touched her hand that first day, here on the sidewalk; but since then, including the time he had seen her at her own house, the whole idea of Dora had seemed unreal to him. She had been like a form or a shape that he could have put his hand through. Now, having seen her together with the little girl and the husband-father, he knew that Dora was as tangible as Farrell, who now stood with his hand on the headstall of the wagon horse closest to the street.

Monte stood by his horse for a moment, absorbing what he had seen. He loosened the front cinch on the horse and wrapped the reins around the hitching rail. Looking back, he saw that Lurie had handed his wife up into the wagon and was now hauling himself aboard. Farrell let go of the horse and climbed up on the other side. The hired man gathered the reins, turned the horses out into the street, made a sharp turn around, and headed the wagon out of town.

Monte stepped up onto the sidewalk and turned to look around. He realized he had been distracted and hadn't gotten a look at the whole street.

He felt a jolt in his stomach as his gaze traveled down the street to his right. In front of the livery stable were Elswick and Thrall. No wonder Farrell had cut the horses right around. There had been more to ignore than just a Three-Bar cowhand.

Elswick, seated on a large sorrel horse, gave Monte a three-quarter profile. Monte had recognized the dark coat and tall hat as well as the general outline, which was almost identical to the image Monte had seen when Pool was shooting prairie dogs. Now, instead of holding Pool's horse, Elswick was holding Thrall's, a dark brown horse with a blaze.

Thrall, on the ground next to the horse, was bent over by the front left hoof. He had a can of dark grease in his left hand, and with the two forefingers of his right hand he was smearing grease onto the horse's hoof. He had already daubed the left rear hoof, and now he was finishing the front one. He was wearing the sack coat and shotgun chaps, which, together with his low hat, made him look like a mastiff even when he straightened up.

He ducked under the reins and turned to work on the right front hoof. He reached his free right hand around back to hitch up his chaps, then bent to his work. A fleeting glance must have made him take a second look, for he glanced up from his stooped position. He gave a scowl that was visible at fifty yards, then dipped his fingers into the can of grease and went back to work.

Monte looked at Elswick, who did not turn around. The man sat with his back to the world, watching his hired man work. It reminded Monte of a scene he had once observed on the outskirts of Cheyenne. A black collie had been sitting upright, watching, as a brown-and-white spaniel dug furiously into the earth with only its tail end sticking up. It had been an amusing scene at the time.

After giving another glance up and down the street, Monte turned and walked into the café. Ramona was busy with a ranch family at the middle table on his right, so he walked to the left table in back. Taking off his hat and coat, he sat facing the door.

Ramona smiled on the way to the kitchen. "Coffee?"

"Yes, please."

As she poured the coffee, she asked in a low voice, "Did you see them?"

Monte was glad he had looked around, or he might have thought she meant the Luries. "Yes, I did."

Still in a low voice, she said, "I hope they don't come in."

"I doubt that they will, but if they think I'm alone, they might wait for me out of town."

Her face showed a worried look. "Are you?"

"Oh, no. Johnny'll come by lookin' for me in a while, like always."

She glanced at the door and back at him.

"Don't worry," he said. "They left the worst one somewhere else."

She let out a breath. "I guess it's not so bad, then." She looked at the other table and then back at Monte. "Would you like something to eat?"

"No, thanks. I really just came to visit." He gave her a close look. "You know, I thought of something since I was here last."

"Oh, what was that?"

"You probably made pies right after I left."

She laughed. "Actually, since I spent a little time with you, I waited until the next day."

"But there's none left now, I bet."

She lifted her chin. "No, not anymore."

He winked. "Do I have to come in here every day, then?"

She had a playful look on her face as she turned from side to side with her hands together in front of her. "I guess so."

"Well, we'll just have to see."

She stood for a long moment without speaking. Then she said, "Excuse me for a few minutes," and went into the kitchen.

Monte drank his coffee a sip at a time, keeping his eye on the front part of the café. After several minutes he saw the upper portions of Elswick, Thrall, and their horses moving to the left. Not long after that, the ranch family began shuffling chairs and standing up. Monte had the sense that Ramona had gone out the back door to whatever was beyond the kitchen, but in a moment she came out to settle with the man of the family. She cleared the dishes and wiped the table, then disappeared into the kitchen again. Monte felt a little thrill each time she walked past him, and he wished she would stay long enough to talk. Then he heard her voice.

"I have something to show you."

He turned and saw her standing by the kitchen door.

"In here," she said.

He got up and walked to the kitchen. Inside the doorway on the right, leaning against the door-jamb, stood a rifle.

"I didn't want to take it out there," she said.

"It's just as well." He looked at the rifle without touching it. It was a lever-action Winchester, a popular model, and just like the one he had traded to

Weaver. He looked at her. "Is it yours?"

"Yes. It was my husband's."

"It looks like it's in good condition. That's a good rifle."

"I don't use it. I don't know how." She looked serious again.

"Did you want me to show you? Teach you how to shoot it?"

"No," she said as her eyes met his. "I want you to have it."

"You mean—"

"Yes. I want to give it to you."

He looked at the rifle and then at her. "I don't know if that would be right. This thing is worth a bit of money."

"I don't care how much it's worth. I don't use it, and you can. You told me you didn't have one."

"Well, that's true."

"Then let me give it to you. You gave me a nice gift, and I want to give you something."

His eyes widened. "Ramona, I mean, something like this is worth a lot more than—"

"I see them as being worth the same. Can't you?"

"Well, I guess so. But they seem to be so different."

"They're both gifts," she insisted.

He remembered her reluctance a few days earlier, and he remembered how he had felt. That was how she would be feeling now. He wanted her to feel happy as he had.

"Thank you, Ramona," he said. He took the rifle and held it, barrel straight up, and admired it. "This is a beautiful gift," he said, looking at her, "and all

149

the more so because it's from you." He set the rifle back against the doorjamb. "Thank you," he said. He bent to kiss the back of her hand, and she did not take it away. He lifted his head and met her eyes with his.

Her dark eyes were shining. "You're welcome."

Chapter Ten

Johnny was surprised to see the rifle. When he learned that Monte had acquired it from the woman Ramona, he didn't ask any more questions.

"You'll want to try it out, though," he said as Monte tied it to the saddle. Johnny looked at the sky. "I bet we have time to drop by Riggs's new camp on the way home."

Monte spoke in a low voice. "Might not be a bad idea. I'd just as soon take a different way home anyway. I saw Elswick and Thrall right after you and I split up, and they might think I'm alone."

Johnny pursed his lips and swung into the saddle.

Monte turned his horse into the street and climbed aboard also. "But, as I mentioned to Ramona, they didn't have the worst one with 'em."

Johnny gave a small laugh and said, not very

loud, "So she fixed you up with a rifle just in case, uh?"

Monte shrugged. "She said she didn't use it, and she knew I needed one."

"Now, that's a good kind of girl."

Monte smiled. "Just mighty fine, I'd say."

They left town and angled southeast away from the main trail. Monte had a general idea of where the camp would be, as Earl Riggs had told him it would be on the next creek north of their earlier camp. Johnny would know the creek easily enough as they came from the other direction.

They saw the camp from half a mile away as they approached it at a forty-five-degree angle. Like the earlier camp, it consisted of the wall tent, the wagon, and a fire pit, all set at the edge of a small creek. The wagon and tent lay parallel to the creek on the north side, and the fire pit sat between the wagon and the creek. Monte imagined that the tent and wagon made a good south-facing camp and offered some protection when the wind blew. Out from the camp about two hundred yards, the two horses grazed on their picket ropes.

It was a peaceful, quiet scene, with the pale autumn sunlight slanting down on the drab colors of the landscape. The white tent stood out as a sign of human habitation, and a wisp of smoke rising from the campfire suggested that someone was in camp.

From about a hundred yards out, Johnny hollered. One of the brothers came around the end of the wagon and waved them in. A minute later, the other one appeared and also waved. Then they went back into their camp and out of sight.

Drawing closer, Monte saw four carcasses hanging on the shady north side of the wagon. It looked as if the Riggs brothers were still in business.

Earl came back into the open as the riders came within fifty feet of the wagon. "Fall off and sit awhile," he said after they had all said hello.

Monte and Johnny tied their horses to the two front wheels of the wagon and then followed Earl into the camp. George was sitting cross-legged on the ground, sharpening a sheath knife on a whetstone. He looked up, smiling, and exchanged greetings with the visitors.

Johnny squatted on the ground next to him and said, "Have you killed 'em all yet, George?"

"Not the way the wind's been blowin'. We went out and got four today, though." George dropped a gob of spittle on the stone and spread it with his knife blade. "What day is this? Sunday, isn't it?"

"Uh-huh. Me an' Monte are out doin' our social calls." Johnny looked up at Earl. "Monte has a new rifle he'd like to try out."

Earl's teeth showed as he smiled. "That's what it looked like." He turned to Monte. "Need a scabbard, uh?"

Monte nodded. "Johnny says we can find one back at the ranch."

Earl looked at his brother and then back at Monte. "Well, I can take you out. You want to practice on a live target?"

"Oh, that's not necessary. Any kind of target'll do."

"Well, let me get my horse, and we'll go a ways out."

He went around the tail end of the wagon and out toward the horses. Monte waited at the end of the wagon, where he saw a freshly peeled pole about two inches thick and four feet long leaning against the tailgate. Ten yards away he saw a pile of curled strips of bark, smooth and dark like chokecherry. He imagined George had just peeled the pole for some purpose in their camp.

Earl came back with the horse and tied him to the off rear wheel. He brushed the horse in a minute, then reached into the wagon and hauled out a saddle blanket, which he slapped onto the horse. Next he brought out the saddle, complete with breast collar and empty scabbard. He slung the saddle onto the horse and settled it in place. After cinching down the saddle he reached back into the wagon and pulled out a rifle, which he poked into the scabbard. Next he tied on a rope and changed the halter for a bridle.

"I'm ready," he said.

He and Monte led their horses out from camp and mounted up. Earl led the way east and then crossed the creek, rode up a little rise, and continued east. The land was flat for a mile around, so Monte figured Earl was trying to find him an antelope.

After about twenty minutes of slow riding, Earl stopped his horse. "There's one," he said, pointing to his left. "Sun's at our back, too. That's good."

Monte looked across the ears of Earl's horse and saw an antelope down in a swale about two hundred yards away. From a distance, a young antelope didn't look much different from a grown-up doe. "Is that a young one?" he asked.

Earl had a cheerful tone to his voice. "Yeah, I think so. Looks like a stray." He made a small clicking sound in the corner of his mouth and then said, "Probably lost its mother."

Monte laughed. "You mean it might be hangin' upside-down in your camp."

Riggs, still looking at the antelope, raised his eyebrows and smiled as he nodded. Then he looked at Monte and said, "Go ahead and take a shot if you want. We can sure use the meat if you don't want it."

Monte didn't feel much enthusiasm. "Oh, I don't care if I shoot it or not."

Riggs looked at him again. "Really?"

Monte shook his head. "Nah, go ahead if you want."

"Hell, meat's meat. Do you want to hold the horses?"

"Sure." Monte dismounted and took the other reins. He stood with one set of reins in each hand.

Earl pulled out his rifle and walked forward in a crouch. He stretched himself out in a prone position, took slow aim, and touched off a shot. All together the rifle boomed, the horses jumped, and the antelope snapped to the ground.

Earl pushed himself to his feet and turned around. "Good, clean shot," he said as he poked the gun into the scabbard.

They rode down into the swale where the antelope lay, its white belly shining in the sunlight. It had not kicked once.

"I'll get it myself," said Earl as he swung down with his rope in hand. Holding his reins, he bent down and picked up the hind legs of the animal. He snugged the loop of his rope over both hocks, then threw two more hitches behind the loop. He straightened up and played out the rope. Then, with the horse facing the antelope, he climbed back into the saddle. He swung the horse around so that the rope lay across his right thigh, and as the horse walked away he snugged the rope to his saddle horn.

Monte looked down as the animal flopped into place. He saw that the bullet had gone through the base of the neck. It was a good clean shot, all right. Riggs knew his work. Monte didn't care to shoot a young antelope himself, but as Riggs had said, meat was meat. Monte guessed it was not that much different from the cattle business, except that cattle were bigger and they went away to the slaughterhouse.

"We're close enough to camp that we can drag him back there, where I can hang him up and jerk that hide in a few seconds. Cool it out quick, and none of the meat goes to waste."

The horses picked up a good walk, and Riggs seemed happy. "These little lambs are good eatin'," he said. "You want to take some back to your cook?"

"Nah, that's all right." Monte looked back at the carcass as it scuffed along. It probably was good eating, but it was Riggs's meat.

Riggs, still cheerful, dragged the antelope through the creek. The water was down to a narrow stream, so the animal touched water only once as the horse scrambled up the other side.

Riding up toward camp, Monte saw a third man seated by the campfire. Closer now, Monte recognized the slouch hat and relaxed posture. It was Conde. He and the other two men were engaged in what appeared to be an amiable conversation. Conde waved as Earl and Monte rode around to the back side of the wagon. Monte waved back, as did Earl; Monte sensed that the Riggs brothers had already made Conde's acquaintance.

By the time Monte had tied up his horse, Earl had freed his rope and stripped his horse. Monte offered to put the horse back on picket, which he did. When he came back, Earl had skinned the hocks and hung the antelope on the side of the wagon. He was skinning the hindquarters now, exposing the pink meat. Faint wisps of steam rose in the cool air.

Earl gave the hide a steady downward pull and brought it down to the brisket, where he gave a few swipes with his knife before pulling the hide down to the neck and legs. Monte noticed he had already cut off the forelegs. Earl trimmed a few more licks, pulled each leg out of the hide, which was inside out, and draped the hide over the head. His knife seemed to find the right joint, as it severed the head from the neck with no trouble and left the head attached to the hide.

Earl straightened up now and cut open the carcass, spilling out the viscera in steamy loops and bulges. His hands seemed to work by themselves, and in a few minutes he had the carcass clean and

157

empty. Bending over again, he stretched out the hide and head so that the piece was hairy-side-out again. He held the hide like a gunnysack and tucked the innards inside, then tossed in the forelegs and dragged away the mess in one package.

Monte walked around the wagon to join the other men. They all had tin cups, and a bottle sat on the ground between them. Conde, who was nearest to Monte, looked up and smiled. As before, he looked harmless with his large brown eyes and soft chin. Monte nodded to him.

"Care for a nip?" George sang out. He was sitting between the other two.

"Oh, I suppose I could."

George came to his feet. "I've got one more cup. Earl can use mine when he gets here."

Monte sat down on the other side of Johnny and took a look at Conde. It was hard to imagine him having much to do with Weaver's death.

Conde tipped up his cup and brought it down, wincing and then licking his lips. "He can have mine," he said. "I ought to be going." He pushed himself up and onto his feet. "The sun hastens westward," he said with a smile and a dip of his head. He tipped his hat to George and the boys on the ground. "Thanks, George. So long, gents."

He gathered his horse and walked it out of camp. A little farther on he stopped to talk to Earl, who was washing his hands downstream. Then he mounted up, splashed through the creek, and headed off to the southeast.

Earl came back to camp, wiping his hands on his

shirt. "Conde didn't stay long," he said as he sat down.

"He wanted you to have his cup." George handed his brother a cup and the bottle.

"I don't think he's that shy, especially when it's someone else's bottle." Earl tipped a few glugs into the cup.

Johnny spoke. "I think he wanted to get back before someone came lookin' for him."

Earl took a sip. "Hell, he's been here before." Then he looked at Monte and Johnny. "Oh, uh-huh. With you two he'd be fraternizin', I suppose."

"I guess so," Johnny said. "Someone would see it that way." He paused and looked around the circle. "I don't suppose you boys have heard about Weaver, Lurie's man."

The Riggs brothers looked at each other and back at Johnny, shaking their heads.

"Well, I doubt you'd have heard it from him," Johnny said. He went on to tell about the incident in Weaver's camp and what followed.

When he had finished the story, Monte spoke. "To Conde's credit, I will say that I don't think he had anything to do with it. I don't think he even knew why they were comin' into the camp to begin with, and I don't think he went back later."

"I don't think so, either," Johnny said. "If he had, he wouldn't have stayed now when he saw me."

George spoke next. "I think he probably stayed as long as he could. It seems to me as if he's tryin' to make friends without his boss knowin' it."

Earl cleared his throat. "I don't think he likes it

where he is, and if he wants to get out, he might need some friends."

"He'll make 'em faster by himself than he will with them others," Johnny said.

The four men sat and drank and talked for a while longer. When there was a lull in the conversation, Monte and Johnny looked at each other.

"About time, I suppose," Monte said.

"You could stay and eat a bean," George offered.

Johnny stood up and brushed off his woolly chaps. "Thanks, George, but I think we'd better be goin'."

Monte stood up also, as did the brothers. He thanked them for the drink.

"Anytime," Earl said. "Come back again."

"Likewise," said Johnny. "If you hear somethin', don't be shy."

As Monte and Johnny led the horses out, Earl spoke again.

"You didn't get to try out your new rifle, did you?"

"Nah, but that's all right," Monte said. "I'll find another chance soon enough."

The weather stayed calm through the next morning. Thane sent the boys out to see if anything looked different since the week before. They rode out and around but saw nothing unusual. By noon they were at the farthest point southeast on their ride, so they stopped in a dry wash to have a bite to eat.

Monte sat looking south at the other side of the draw. "You know," he said, "that cutbank would be a good place to shoot into, to see if this rifle is on target."

Johnny stuck out his lower lip. "I suppose so. Couldn't do any harm. We haven't seen anyone all day." He raised his eyebrows. "If I had an ace of spades I'd set it up for you, but I'm all out."

"That's all right," Monte said. "I can use some of this catalogue paper." He reached into his pocket, took out his supply, and unfolded it. He tore off a piece about four inches by six and put the rest back in his pocket.

He walked across the draw, picking up a flat rock on the way. He used the rock to scratch out a little ledge, then tucked the paper onto the shelf and pegged it down with the rock. He knelt to the level of his target and looked back to the north, finding a spot that would give him a clear line of sight. Fixing the spot in his mind, he walked back to Johnny, who was standing with the horses.

"I want to shoot from up there," he said. "You probably want to stay behind me." He pulled the rifle from the scabbard and led the way.

Looking first for cactus, he stretched out on his stomach. The sheepskin coat felt bulky, so he sat up and took it off, then spread it out for a place to rest his elbows. He levered in a shell and settled into position. Seeing that he had a good line of fire, he lowered the end of the rifle until the bead lined up with the notch of the rear sight. The paper was barely bigger than the bead. He squeezed the trigger.

The rifle bit into his shoulder with the recoil as the sound crashed through the air. He looked at

Johnny, levered in a new cartridge, and settled into position again. This time he held the stock tighter against his shoulder. When the bead was steady on the speck of paper, he fired again. No dust had risen with either shot.

"Let's go see," he said, rising with the rifle in his right hand and the coat in his left. He handed the rifle to Johnny while he put on his coat. Then he walked, with Johnny and the horses following, down to his target.

Both shots had hit the paper. One shot had clipped the upper left-hand corner, and the other shot was fairly close on center. Monte handed the paper to Johnny.

"Shoots all right," Monte said. "I held it tighter on the second shot. I hope that was the one that hit the center."

"Either one is a good shot." Johnny looked back up at the hillside. "A little over a hundred yards, you figure?"

"I think so." As Monte turned to put the rifle into his scabbard, he saw movement to the northeast.

Two riders were approaching.

"Looks like we attracted some company," he said, keeping the rifle in his hands.

Johnny turned and looked. "Sure does. And you know who it looks like."

Monte did. As the riders came closer he recognized the dark outlines of Elswick and Pool.

The riders came forward, slower now and ten yards apart. Monte said in a low voice, "You keep an eye on Elswick, and I'll keep an eye on Pool." Then he realized that was a mistake, as both Pool and Johnny were on his right. "No," he said, "let's do it the other way around. I'll watch Elswick."

"All right." Johnny moved aside with his horse and put the reins in his left hand.

Monte stood in front of his own horse with the reins in his left hand as well. He held the rifle in his right, pointing the barrel at the ground.

Elswick's voice came out before the riders stopped. "Heard some shootin'. Thought we'd come and see what it was."

Monte saw the lean features and the clipped mustache beneath the tall, dark hat. The overhead sun cast a shadow on Elswick's face and glinted on his silver watch chain. The riders had stopped now. Elswick had his right hand on his saddle horn, and Monte could see he wasn't wearing gloves.

Monte glanced at Pool, who also had his gloves off. He had taken out his thin-bladed jackknife and was trimming his fingernails, making a show of ignoring the two men on the ground as he kept his hands in view.

"Just practicing," Monte said.

"Is that right? What for?"

The knife blade glinted, but Monte tried to keep his eyes on Elswick. "Hunting," he said. "I notice the Riggs boys are prospering."

"Good for them."

Monte noticed that both horses were shining with sweat. Elswick and Pool must have been moving at a good pace. Monte took a deliberate look at the front quarters of Elswick's horse and then looked up at the man. "Warm weather," he said.

Elswick's mouth tightened and then he spoke. "Not so much."

Monte remembered Elswick's tendency to contradict and challenge, but he said nothing. He let the silence hang in the air.

"We've been on a hard ride," Elswick went on. "Chasin' a horse that got away."

"He must be gone, then."

"He'll slow down, and we'll pick up his trail again. We just thought we'd ride over to see what the noise was."

"Well, I guess you know now."

Elswick's head seemed to go back a quarter of an inch. "I know what you told me." He looked at Johnny. "You ride for Thane, don't you?"

Johnny nodded. "That's right, sir."

Elswick looked back at Monte. "Do you ride for him too, then?"

"Yes, I do. That's why I've got a Three-Bar horse." Monte looked at Pool, whose snake eyes flickered and then went out of sight as he lowered his hat brim again.

"Uh-huh." Elswick seemed to be thinking it over.

Monte felt himself getting irked at the pretense. By acting as if he didn't know Monte worked for Thane, Elswick was as much as saying he had heard nothing from Thrall about the run-in at Weaver's camp. Monte told himself to stay calm; then he thought of something to say that Elswick couldn't contradict.

"I went to work for him right after I met you that first day."

"I see." Elswick looked at Johnny and then at

Pool. "Well, we've sidetracked long enough. We'll be going."

"So long," said Johnny.

"So long," Monte echoed.

Elswick touched his hat and turned his horse around. Pool folded his knife with a click but did not move his hand toward his pocket until he had turned his horse away.

As Monte noted the wide-brimmed hat, the sallow complexion, and the large-roweled spurs, he realized again that he had not heard Pool's voice.

When the two had ridden off, Monte turned and looked at Johnny. "Well, I don't think they were following us."

"No, I don't think so. They're up to something else today."

Chapter Eleven

Thane showed interest as he heard the story that evening after supper. "No telling what they were up to," he said. "But it's a good thing the two of you were together." He stroked the side of his beard. "I don't like the idea that Weaver was killed and nobody has done anything about it. We can't just say that a certain party is responsible, even if we're dead certain he is. Now with Lurie shorthanded, he's afraid they might make another move against him."

Johnny tapped the seam of his cigarette where he had just licked it. "Does Farrell have someone to ride out with him?"

"Not that I know of. Horace and I are going to ride up there tomorrow so I can have another talk with Lurie. Maybe by the end of the week we'll send you boys out with Farrell." Thane tamped his pipe.

"Meanwhile, Horace wants some deer meat, so you boys can go to work on that in the morning." The boys looked at Horace.

"This is good weather for it," he said. "It'll keep well, and it'll make good stew. Steaks, too, of course." He pointed at the wall where Thane's hat hung on its nail with the white crown sticking forward. "I'd like to put a set of antlers over there, so get a buck if you can find one."

Johnny blew two streams of smoke out of his nose. "I suppose we should plan to be out two days, like before. Take a horse to carry the camp, and another to pack the meat back." He looked at Monte. "There's more deer off to the west."

Monte nodded. It had looked like good deer country in that direction. Furthermore, they shouldn't have to worry about running into any troublemakers.

Later on that evening, as the boys lay stretched out on their bunks, Johnny said, "You can tell the Old Man wants to get this other business wrapped up."

"Seems like it."

"He's got other things to do."

Monte looked across at Johnny. "Oh?"

"Uh-huh. Like last winter. He went to a couple of places back east to do some visitin'. He'd been writin' letters."

"Oh."

"He either didn't find anything to his likin', or he didn't fine a young lass willin' to move out here, so he's workin' on it again this year."

"Can't blame him for that."

"No, not at all. Like Horace says, he'd better do it before he gets too old."

"Does Horace write letters, too?"

"Not that I know of. He said that about the Old Man." Johnny grinned. "Not in front of him, of course."

"For as much as Thane wants to get things wrapped up, he doesn't seem to mind sending us out on this hunting trip."

"Might as well, while the weather's decent. It'll keep Horace happy. Then I imagine he'll send us out to take another look at this other business when we get back."

After breakfast the next morning, the boys went right to work at getting their camp gear together. They carried bedrolls and duffel bags to the barn, where Johnny took down a canvas roll that had been hanging from a rafter.

"The tent," he said. "We'll cut us a center pole when we get there." He went to the toolroom and came back with a hatchet, which he laid on the tent bundle. "What else?"

"Maybe some grub."

"Horace'll bring that out in a little bit. I suppose we can get the horses."

They brought in the two packhorses first and fitted them out with packsaddles. Horace appeared, wearing a hat and coat and carrying a rolled-up flour sack with both hands. Monte took the bundle, and it felt heavier than it looked.

"There's a skillet in there," Horace said. "For the bacon. And there's biscuits and canned peaches and cold meat. I figured you'd want one hot meal at least. And there's coffee, of course."

Johnny looked up from sorting the gear into two piles. "How 'bout a coffeepot?"

"Take the one from the chuck wagon, but make sure it gets put back."

The boys thanked Horace and went back to packing. They wrapped each half of the load in canvas sheets and then tied on those two bundles. Then they tied the food on top, nestled between the tops of the other two packs. As usual, Johnny took the lead whenever he could. Monte didn't mind, as he was well used to it by now and he enjoyed watching Johnny throw the hitches and snug down the ropes.

Johnny plucked at the lashes on the pack and seemed satisfied. "We'll throw a bag of grain on that other one so he won't think he's on a holiday. Then we can saddle up and be gone."

The sky was hazy and the morning was still cold when they rode out of the ranch. Johnny led the packhorse with the camp, while Monte led the other one. The smell of wood smoke carried on the air as they climbed the slope north of the bunkhouse. Monte saw the long shadows of the horses on the dry grass, and he felt the rifle in its scabbard beneath his left leg.

"Not much of a moon last night," Johnny said. "Should be better for huntin'."

They rode westward, going up and down hills but gradually climbing in elevation. After about an hour they stopped on a high point to give the horses a breather.

Monte turned in the saddle to look at the country

spread out below. He had been up this far before, looking for cedar wood, but the country made more sense now that he had been down and around in it. He saw the hills and buttes in the distance, and the pine ridge to the south. He could not see the Three-Bar ranch, but he had a good idea of where it was. Several miles to the north of that spot, he thought he could see the cluster of roofs that would make up Eagle Spring. In between, and farther out on the scattered plain, he guessed at where the other places would be—Weaver's camp, Riggs' camp, the two places where he had seen Elswick and Pool. Somewhere out there, he thought, Elswick's men might be going about their devious business. It was better to think of Ramona, off to the left in Eagle Spring. It was nice to think of her like this, when he was out in the open country. It made the country look more benevolent.

"Pretty, isn't it?" he said out loud.

"Sure is," Johnny answered.

"I bet it's pretty when it's green, too."

"Oh, it is. But I like this time of year."

"Uh-huh. You're not on the run. You have time to stop and see things."

"That, and you don't have any flies."

Monte looked at the two packhorses, both with their heads lowered as if they had dozed off. "I suppose we should check the packs," he said. Then he noticed that Johnny was rolling a cigarette, so he swung down. "I'll do it," he said.

The sun had climbed in the east but hadn't warmed the air very much or lifted the haze. Monte checked the lashes and then loafed around looking down at the country until Johnny finished his cigarette.

They rode on, still moving higher a little at a time. The earth was redder now in the gashes and bare spots, and rocks lay on the surface of the ground. At midmorning the boys dropped down to the left and watered the horses at the creek. They had been following the creek since they left the ranch, but they had stayed on higher ground to avoid the creek bed with its deadfall and rocks and occasional canyons.

Monte crouched at the edge of the creek upstream from the horses. Taking off his hat and gloves and setting them aside, he dipped cold water with his cupped hands, then splashed his face. It was bracing cold, and it made him feel strong. He splashed himself again, then smoothed down his mustache and rocked on his heels.

"Cold?" asked Johnny, who was holding the horses and smoking a cigarette.

"Just right."

When Johnny had finished his cigarette and thrown the pinched end into the water, the riders got moving again. They hadn't seen any cattle for over an hour. Monte mentioned it, and Johnny said that just about all the cattle had come down with the first storm they had had, about three weeks earlier.

"I wouldn't be surprised to see a dead one or two," he said. "That storm hit fast and blew hard."

A little later on they did find a dead animal. They heard the racket of crows and followed the noise. Down in a draw leading to the creek lay a brindle cow, gaunt and pecked out but not very dry.

"Not one of ours," said Johnny, wrinkling his nose.

In the afternoon they pitched their camp along the creek. Monte started a fire while Johnny grained the horses and put them out to graze. Then the two of them set up the tent and laid out their bedrolls and bags inside. It was a pyramid tent, not much different from Weaver's. They hung the saddles in a low cottonwood, stashed the rifles in the tent, and settled in to relax. Evening came on quickly in the shadow of the mountains.

They warmed the cold beef in the skillet, divided it up, and ate it with cold biscuits. All was quiet and peaceful, with only the sound of the stream gurgling by. They had not seen another person all day, nor a recent camp or any recent rubbish. The range country and its problems seemed down below and far way, yet Monte thought about those things. He remembered Weaver, Elswick and his men, and even Conde. It would all be there when they got back.

Johnny must have been thinking about some of the same things. After gazing into the fire for a long while, he spoke. "It seemed like Mrs. Lurie already knew you."

Monte was surprised by the question but not bothered. "She did. We knew each other in Cheyenne when we were growing up."

"Oh."

"Not much to it, really."

"No, I suppose not. Everyone comes from somewhere." Johnny fiddled with a twig and then threw it into the fire. "I wouldn't pass any remarks around Farrell, though."

"I hadn't planned to. Is he pretty touchy?"

"With anything about the Luries, he is. And it sounds like we'll be ridin' with him."

"Well, that's a thought. Thanks for mentionin' it."

In the morning, Monte built up the fire while Johnny took the horses to water and fed them grain. Monte sliced the bacon and laid the pieces in the skillet. He and Johnny had agreed to cook early in the day in case they shot a deer and wanted to break camp without a lot of delay.

"Fire feels good," Johnny said as he hunkered down. He looked around and grinned. "Didn't you want to splash your face this morning?"

"I already did."

After breakfast, the boys took their rifles from the tent and set out on foot, having taken off their spurs in camp. They knew to look for deer in the sunny places on a cold morning, so they climbed up above the creek and split up.

The first little climb had warmed him up, so Monte walked slowly now. As he saw a line of trees angling down the hillside above him, he reasoned that it was a drainage leading to the creek where they were camped. He decided to follow that draw and keep an eye on the sunny side.

Looking back, he saw the horses and the camp. He remembered how dark it had been the night before. He had gone out behind the tent before going to bed, and he had seen five white spots on the ground a ways out from camp. It had taken him a

173

couple of minutes of watching how the spots moved to decide they were the four white socks and white chin of the horse Johnny had been riding.

He looked up. The moon was a faint sliver in the west, and the sun was up in the east. The deer would be out.

He followed the draw to the northwest, walking a little ways and then stopping to take things in. The trees were mixed here, leafless cottonwoods and chokecherries with an occasional cedar. He walked in the shade of the draw, above where most of the trees grew. It was quieter walking with fewer leaves to step on, but he had to look harder to see through the trees.

Twice he thought he saw the right color, but both times it turned out to be a rock. Then he saw color and form, and he felt a jolt go down through him. He lowered to a crouch. It was a deer on the other side of the draw, faced away from him. Monte picked out the slender legs and black tail. He saw the grayish-brown hide glisten as the muscle moved beneath it. The deer was moving a step at a time, grazing along.

Monte took a deep breath to calm himself. If it was a buck, he needed to get good aim. He started a duckwalk but didn't like the balance, so he rose into a stoop and moved forward bent over. The deer was still over a hundred yards away, and Monte had not yet seen its head. He moved softly for another twenty yards and came to rest behind a small cottonwood. With a slow, drawn-out motion he levered a shell into the chamber. He laid his left hand against the tree and rested the forearm of the rifle on his extended thumb.

The deer had its head turned to the left, out of sight. It flicked its black tail. Then it turned its head around, and a set of antlers caught the shine of the morning sun.

Monte lined up the sights on the rib cage in back of the front leg, then squeezed the trigger. The blast of the rifle ripped through the still morning air, and the deer lurched. It ran down into the bottom of the draw, out of sight.

Monte was sure he had made a good hit. Marking the spot where the deer had stood, he moved back up out of the trees and walked along the side of the draw. When he was across from the spot where the deer had last stood, he angled down into the bottom. He went around the left side of a screen of chokecherry trees, and there on the ground before him lay the deer, motionless, with its legs stretched out.

It was a good-sized buck, husky, with long tines on its antlers. It had three points on the right side and two on the left. That should be something for Thane to hang his hat on, and there would be plenty of meat. Monte set the rifle aside and dragged the deer uphill by its antlers. When he had the animal in position he rolled up his sleeves and took out his pocket knife, then went to work at field-dressing the deer.

He had just trimmed out the liver when he heard Johnny's voice.

"I was hopin' that was good news I heard."

Monte rose up and stood back. "What do you

think? Will that be good enough for Horace?"

Johnny pursed his lips and nodded. "For all the work it cost him personally, he ought to think it's dandy."

With the help of their saddle horses, the boys dragged the deer back to camp. They hung it in the cottonwood where they had hung their saddles. As it was cooling, they rolled up their gear and packed the first packhorse. Without a saw to take off the antlers with a skull plate, they decided to load the animal in one piece onto the packhorse. They had to tie up a front leg to keep the horse still, but finally they got the deer tied on, with its head twisted back and the antlers tied to the sawbuck.

Monte remembered once again the assurance he had heard from Conde, that the little sorrel would pack out anything he shot, as long as it was dead. He wondered where the horse was, and he imagined Lurie had taken care of things fairly.

"That's a pretty good load," he said. "He'll earn his oats going back down."

"Everybody has to work," Johnny said with a laugh. "It's not all whiskey and women."

The sun was straight up when they left camp, and their shadows stretched out way ahead of them when they came down the last slope into the ranch. They hung the deer in the barn, then stripped the horses and turned them out.

Monte noticed four new horses in the corral. "I wonder where those came from," he said.

"I think they're Lurie's. I wouldn't be surprised if Farrell brought 'em down so he wouldn't have to ride ours."

Johnny's guess was right. Farrell was waiting in the bunkhouse. He didn't say much, but at supper Monte found out he had ridden in that afternoon. Thane told the men they could ride out all three together in the morning and look over the country where his and Lurie's cattle ran together the most.

The next two days were humorless and uneventful. Farrell hardly ever spoke or showed any expression, but his pale blue eyes were always working. He seemed to know every cow of Lurie's. "That one's dry," he would say. "She didn't have a calf this year." On another occasion he saw a cow by herself and said, "That one should have a calf with her. A heifer calf." He rode for an hour on his own until he rejoined the other two riders. "I found it," he said. "It's all right."

They rode past the site of Weaver's camp without a comment, although earlier in the day Farrell had reminded Johnny of a spot where they had camped during roundup. On the second day, they rode past a quarter-section that had a strip plowed around it to mark a homestead claim. One side of the claim fronted on a stream, where they watered the horses.

As they rode away with Farrell in the lead, Johnny said, "That's your claim, isn't it?"

It was as if someone had asked him if it was Friday. "Yeah," he said without turning around.

On Saturday morning he pulled out and went back to the Circle-L, riding one horse and leading the other three. It had not been hard for Monte to refrain from saying anything personal to him. That evening at supper, after Monte and Johnny had ridden out south for a look around, Thane made a remark.

"Farrell didn't talk your ear off, did he?"

"Not that I noticed," Johnny answered.

"No problems, though?"

Monte and Johnny both answered. "No, none at all."

"That's good. I think he'll be back on Monday morning, and you can work with him for another day or two."

Sunday came around again, and Horace had a little chore. The deer hide and head had been draped on a stanchion in the barn since the boys had skinned the deer, and Horace wanted them to saw off the antlers and get rid of all the rest. Nothing had begun to smell in the cold weather, so the boys had been in no hurry to tend to that detail. Now they did as Horace asked them, peeling the hide off the skull plate as well. Then they mounted the antlers on the wall inside the cookhouse door.

Horace was pleased, and he showed his appreciation by fixing a dinner of venison steak and gravy. After dinner, Thane said he had some letter writing to do, and Horace said he was going to bake bread. Monte and Johnny were free to go to town, so they made short work of getting ready. They decided to take ranch horses and go directly to and from town.

A breeze was stirring when they left, making the air cold and dry. They rode into town without much talk. When they got there, Johnny went his usual way and Monte went his.

The main street was nearly deserted, so there was

little to distract his attention as he rode to the café. Ramona was looking out the window as he turned his horse in and tied it to the hitching rail.

She met him at the door as he walked in. She had a soft expression on her face as she said, "It's good to see you."

"Well, it's nice to see you," he said, letting his glance rove and then meeting her eye. "How are you doing?"

"Just fine," she answered. "Maybe a little bored, actually. No one has come in since this morning."

He took off his hat. "Do you ever get tired of being in here all day, every day?"

She let out a breath. "Oh, yes, I do. But for right now, there doesn't seem to be another way."

He looked outside. "It's not too bad out. If things are slow, would you like to go out for a walk?"

Her face brightened. "I think it would do me some good. Let me get my coat."

He stood with his hat in his hand and watched her walk away. She came back, smiling, and he put his hat on. He opened the door for her and then closed it as he stepped outside.

"Where shall we walk?" he asked as he handed her down into the street.

"Oh, anywhere." She gave a short laugh that sounded weary. "There's really not anywhere to go."

"Well, we could walk out north a ways to the end of town, then come around in back of the stable and say hello to your horse."

"That would be fine."

She had her hands in her pockets again, so he walked with his hands at his side.

"It's good just to be outside," she said.

He liked hearing her say that. He remembered having thought of her as he looked at the landscape from up in the foothills. "Do you like to go riding?" he asked.

"Yes, I do. Sometimes. But I don't think we could today. I would need to know ahead of time, and wear the right clothes, and all of that."

"Oh, sure. I didn't really mean today. I thought it might be an idea for next Sunday, maybe, if I have it free."

She looked at him. "That would be all right."

They walked out north, past the edge of town. They talked about what they had been doing, and he told her he had gone hunting with the rifle she had given him. She said she was glad he was able to use it so soon, and he said he was, too.

A ways out from town, they turned and came back on the west side of the main street behind the buildings. They came to a stop at the corral behind the stable, and the bay horse came over to greet them.

Monte saw motion in the sky above; looking up, he saw a flock of geese, again headed north.

Ramona looked up, too, then turned to him and smiled. "They're pretty, aren't they?"

"Yes, they are." Feeling a boldness, he added, "It makes me want to put my arm around you."

She had a slight wince as she looked at him. "Not now. I always feel that someone is watching me here."

Monte looked around. "I don't see anyone, but I know what you mean in a small town." He felt a wave of emotion as he stood next to her. She had taken her hands out of her pockets to pet the horse, and her right hand was close to his left, down between them and out of sight. He moved his hand to hers, and they joined. "I bet I could kiss you quick, once on the cheek, before anyone saw me."

She looked at him sideways and smiled. "I bet you could."

Chapter Twelve

The north wind blew cold. It came through the cracks in the lumber and around the windows; it even came in around the doors on the south side of the bunkhouse. It was not so strong that it howled, but a person inside knew it was blowing. When Monte stepped outside in the predawn dark of Monday morning, he felt the wind. Cold and sharp but not at gale force, it carried the smell of sage, dust, and dry grass.

Shortly after daylight, as the men sat around after breakfast, hoofbeats sounded on the hard earth outside.

"Sounds like horses," said Johnny. " 'Magine that's Farrell."

Horace went to the door and called out an invitation, then closed the door and came back to the table. "He says he'll go put his horses away."

"Well, go ahead, then, boys," Thane said. "He'll probably wait for you there."

Thane was right. Farrell had turned his horses into a separate corral and was waiting inside the barn in the dim light. His war bag and bedroll were sitting on the straw. Monte assumed he would take them in later.

They all said good morning. Monte and Johnny got their ropes and went out to catch horses for the day's work. The horses were skittish and hard to catch, no doubt because of the wind. They ran all together in the corral, switching and sashaying, with their heads up and nostrils open. They would stop with their rumps to the wind and then bolt again. Finally the boys roped the two they wanted and brought them into the barn.

Farrell spoke in his dry voice. "I think we need to go over farther east."

Johnny answered. "Oh, uh-huh."

"I didn't see enough cattle last week," Farrell added.

Johnny slipped a halter onto his horse. "We can do that."

The three men rode out to the northeast, with the wind coming at them at a slant. Half a mile out, Monte remembered they hadn't brought anything to eat. It would be a long day, he thought.

Farrell obviously knew where he wanted to go. He led them straight across country, crossing the main trail and moving on to the south of the Riggs brothers' hunting camps.

"We can work this area," he said. "I'll go north."

The week before, they had established a pattern

for working the country, and they had agreed to meet up at intervals no longer than half an hour, give or take a little. Without anyone saying it today, Monte knew they shouldn't get very far separated.

Johnny took the middle as Monte rode to the south. About a mile to the east, the two of them met up and waited until Farrell joined them. They worked in that pattern through the morning, and it was hard to tell if Farrell was seeing what he wanted. The cattle seemed to be mixed about the same, with maybe a few more of Elswick's over on this part of the range.

After working the range several miles to the east, they rode south a ways and then turned back to the west, riding the same pattern. The sun was crossing overhead, and Monte was feeling hungry. Johnny probably was, too. He called it "dog's lunch" when they had to miss a meal, and he tried not to let it happen. Monte doubted that Farrell gave it much thought, though. He would chew on a toothpick and hardly even drink water.

Monte was about to ride his circle back around to join up when he saw a cow run up over a hill. Thinking that there must be something to cause a cow to run like that, he turned in that direction. Then, at second thought, he decided it might be better if he had company, so he rode back and found Johnny. The two of them rode together to take a look.

When they got to the spot they saw nothing, so they went back and waited for Farrell. The wind still blew cold, and the day was getting long already. Monte had had an uneasy feeling all day, and it wasn't getting any better. Farrell joined them without a word, so they all moved on. In a little while they split up again.

Monte had worked a quarter mile off to his right when he looked back and saw Johnny waving. He put his horse into a trot and headed on over to see what was going on.

Johnny pointed straight ahead where the ground rose to a little ridge, but he did not speak.

Monte nodded, then fell in alongside Johnny and his horse. After a hundred yards more, they dismounted and walked, holding the reins in back of them so the horses could trail behind.

As they topped the rise, Monte saw a cow and a calf jostling along, with Thrall on a horse trotting close behind. He had his rope out, coils in his left hand and loop in his right. From his mouth dangled a piggin' string, a rawhide thong from the looks of it. Monte thought he looked like a dog with a muskrat in his mouth. The cow and calf were Herefords, carrying Circle-L brands. They were moving south, from right to left across Monte's field of vision. Thrall must have had his eyes right on them, for he seemed intent and did not look up.

Johnny glanced at Monte and motioned backward with his head. The two of them sank back.

"Let's let him throw his loop," Johnny said as he felt for his gun. "We've got him."

"All right." Monte touched his own gun to make sure it was in place. He felt his stomach getting nervous, and he hoped Thrall would see the game was up and try not to make things worse.

The Three-Bar riders swung into their saddles

and moved the horses forward. Monte saw the cow running now, with Thrall cutting in between her and her calf. Thrall was swinging his rope, and as the calf took off to its left, Thrall made his throw. He made a good catch, for the loop of the rawhide lariat went down around the calf's ears and nose and settled on its neck. In one motion, Thrall stopped the horse and dropped his slack. The lariat was tied hard and fast to the saddle horn, so the calf ran out to the end of the rope and got jerked off its feet. As Thrall jumped down from the saddle, Monte and Johnny came down the slope on a gallop.

"Hee-yah!" hollered Johnny.

"Hold it right there, Thrall!" Monte shouted.

Thrall pulled his gun and fired in the air, then slipped the gun back into his holster as the boys came off their horses with their guns drawn. Thrall held his hands palm out at his sides. He had let the piggin' string fall to the ground.

"Put 'em away," he said. "I was just ringin' the bell."

"It's a good way to get shot," Johnny said as he holstered his gun.

Thrall's gravelly voice came right back. "It's a good way for you to get shot, comin' up on a man like that."

Monte did not like Thrall's sarcastic tone, but he put away his gun. "You've got some nerve, Thrall," he said. "We saw you rope that calf."

"That one?" Thrall jerked his head toward his right shoulder. "I just wanted to check its brand. It looked like someone had changed it."

He turned around and, reaching for the bridle of his horse, moved the horse forward. Slack went into the lariat, and the calf scrambled to its feet. It had been lying on its left side, covering the brand. As it got up, the Circle-L brand was visible once again.

Monte looked around to see where the mama cow was, and he saw Pool riding down from the other side of the draw. The cow was standing at bay on the other side of Pool and his horse.

Pool had out his knife and a plug of tobacco. He cut off a slice and held it with his thumb against the blade, then slipped the tobacco into his mouth, showing his narrow, gapped front teeth.

The calf was pulling on the rope now. Monte saw that it was a small calf for the fall, like the other one they had found tied up. Still, it would be a handful for one man. Thrall walked down the rope with his left hand on the line, then made a smooth, quick move to the off side. When he got to the calf he reached over for a flank and front leg, then dropped the calf on the ground with its left side up. Sitting on the calf's ribs, he ran his stubby hand over the brand. Then he pulled slack into the rope, loosened the loop on the calf's neck, and stood up. The calf kicked its way onto its feet and ran away.

"Hard to say," Thrall said in his rough voice. "That's the kind you can read best from the inside."

Monte felt himself getting mad at Thrall's insolence. "That's too easy to say," he snapped. "You know it's not your calf. You had no business ropin' it."

"Well, it's not yours either. Seems to me like

187

you're buttin' in again." Thrall stood with his hands on the hips of his shotgun chaps. He stared from beneath his heavy brow, then turned to spit tobacco juice to his left.

Monte wondered if Thrall wanted to take another drubbing. Maybe he wanted a second chance, thinking he could win if he fought a different kind of fight. Maybe he was trying to set something up with Pool standing by. Monte glanced at Pool, who was looking across and behind Johnny Romaine. Monte looked around and saw Farrell coming down the slope. Now it was three to two, he thought. That was better. It didn't look as if Elswick was around; this was not his kind of work. Monte wondered where Conde was, and he hoped the man was off having a nip with the Riggs brothers.

Monte turned back toward Thrall but said nothing.

Thrall wasn't losing his cheeky tone. "Maybe you're buttin' in this time on someone else's behalf."

Monte gave him a narrow look, wondering what he might mean.

Thrall raised his chin. "Like Mrs. Lurie. I heard you were pretty sweet on her once, used to follow her around like a dog. Is that why you're here now?"

Monte felt the blood rush to his face. He clenched his teeth and told himself to stay calm. His mouth was going dry, and he was about to frame an answer when a blur of denim moved in front of him.

It was Farrell, moving with quick steps and landing a smashing blow on Thrall's left cheekbone. As Thrall fell back a couple of steps, Monte glanced at

Pool, who sat with his hands in plain view on his saddle horn. It was going to be a fight.

Thrall's hat had fallen away. Now he took off his coat and tossed it on the ground with his gun. Monte saw again the thick head of bristly hair with its low hairline, the blocky face, the massive chest and shoulders, and the squatty chaps.

Farrell took off his denim coat and tossed it on the ground, then laid his hat and gun on top of it. He looked hard as whipcord as he came at Thrall.

He smashed with his left fist and then his right, rocking Thrall's head but not knocking the man down. Thrall swung back, but Farrell had the reach on him and stayed out of range. Farrell came in to land two more punches, and Thrall caught him once with a right.

Farrell stood back, his pale blue eyes open and searching, as if he was taking aim on the best place to land a fist. He seemed confident, as if he was sure he could hit his opponent wherever he wanted and it was just a matter of where.

He loves Dora, Monte thought. That was where Thrall had made a mistake. He thought he was putting a gig into Monte about being a dog, and he got the real one. Monte looked at Farrell. He was like the kind of dog that men trained to go down into holes and fight badgers.

Farrell moved back into the fight, leading with a left that caught Thrall on the mouth and nose. He moved out, then back in with a left to the jaw. Thrall caught him again with a right to the head, but Farrell showed no effect as he moved back out and waited.

Monte could tell that Farrell knew he was in the right. When a man felt that way, he fought with more confidence. It gave him an edge.

Monte looked at Thrall. Another man might have felt his opponent's edge more keenly, but Thrall didn't seem to. At one time Monte had thought Thrall knew better than to make slurs about decent women, or what he might think were decent women, but now it seemed as if Thrall had little regard for that code. And it was going to get him thrashed.

Thrall's face was glistening now. He had broken a sweat, as he had done in the earlier fight. Monte was sure that Farrell could smell him.

Farrell came in again, working on Thrall's head. He jabbed with the left and clubbed with the right. Then, as Monte expected, Thrall lowered his head and charged at Farrell. He got his arms around Farrell's body and locked his hands behind Farrell's ribs. He gave a fierce hug, but Farrell, who was a head taller than Thrall, bounced with his toes and sprawled outward. He broke Thrall's grasp and pushed him downward and away.

They were both on their feet again and circling. Thrall moved his left foot and then his right, never crossing them. Monte could smell him on the breeze now as he edged closer. Monte saw the left side of Thrall's shiny face, the animal gleam in his squinty eye.

Thrall faked a punch and then rushed Farrell again. Farrell hit Thrall's slick forehead with the heel of his hand, then put both hands on the back of Thrall's head and pulled him forward. Thrall stumbled, and Farrell stepped to the side and shoved him forward to the ground.

Thrall rolled over, came up on all fours, and rose to fight again. His lower lip hung down, and he was breathing heavily through his mouth. He moved toward Farrell again, slower this time and reaching out his meaty hands to grab his opponent. Farrell grabbed his right arm and yanked it, then moved in and grabbed him sideways. He lifted Thrall from the ground, used his right leg to sweep Thrall's legs into the air, and slammed Thrall to the ground.

Farrell stood back as Thrall came up again. The man seemed to have an animal energy with no sense of knowing when to quit. Sweaty and dirty and beaten, he lunged at Farrell with arms flailing. Farrell slammed a hard right fist into Thrall's stomach, which doubled him over. Then Farrell grabbed Thrall's left wrist and upper arm, pulled him forward, and tripped him. Thrall hit the ground flat with his right arm beneath him, and Farrell followed him to the ground and landed with his right knee below Thrall's left shoulder blade.

Thrall gave a horrible heaving gasp and then vomited. Farrell stood up and stepped back as Thrall pushed himself up to his hands and knees and vomited again.

Monte looked away and then remembered Pool. He looked up and around until he saw Pool riding in the direction of Thrall's horse, which had wandered about forty yards away. Monte was pretty sure the fight was over for today. He looked around at Johnny Romaine, who had a sick look on his face as he stood holding Farrell's horse and his own.

Farrell stooped over to pick up his hat, coat, and gun. He looked relatively clean, for he had not hit the ground once. Even so, thought Monte, he had to feel grimy after all that contact with Thrall.

When Farrell had everything in place, he took the reins from Johnny and pulled himself up into the saddle. He rode away without looking back at Thrall or Pool either one. Monte and Johnny mounted up also. Johnny went first, and Monte took a look around to see if they had left anything. Thrall was still on his hands and knees, and Pool was bringing his horse back to him.

Farrell did not say anything for the rest of the day until they rode back into the ranch.

"I think I'll go back tonight," he said.

He picked up his war bag and bedroll and tied them to his saddle as the Three-Bar riders unsaddled their horses. They helped him run his three horses into the barn, where he put lead ropes on them and led them out.

The boys said "So long," and Farrell muttered something as he rode away.

Thane and Horace listened with great interest as Johnny told the story of the incident. He managed to tell it without making direct reference to Thrall's remark about Mrs. Lurie.

"It was a hell of a fight," he said. "They both went back to the animal. Didn't they, Monte?"

"They sure did."

Horace spoke up. "Farrell must feel pretty well wrung out. He should've stayed the night."

"I think he felt he'd had enough," Monte said.

Johnny twisted his mouth and then said, "I bet

Thrall feels he had more than enough. He doesn't know when to quit. But I bet he learned a little somethin' about where to throw his lariat."

"I hope so," Thane said. "You can't blame Farrell, that's for sure. But I hope he didn't make things worse."

The rest of the week was quiet. Farrell did not come back, and as far as Monte knew, no communication passed between Thane and Lurie. Thane sent the boys out each day for the next four days, with the understanding that they would keep to themselves as much as possible.

Johnny's interpretation seemed reasonable. "I think the Old Man has a wait-and-see attitude right now. He wants to see what Elswick is gonna do next, and he wants to wait and hear from Lurie. He'll side with Lurie, but he wants to be sure Lurie'll do the same for him."

The riding had become routine by now, and since they weren't herding or rounding up or doing anything that had an objective—even cutting wood or hunting meat—the days had an aimless quality to them. Monte had plenty of time to think, and impressions from Monday's episode came back time and again.

Perhaps the most insistent impression was his sense of Farrell's loyalty. Lurie's man rode for the brand like any good cowpuncher should, but he seemed to have devoted himself to an abnormal degree. He didn't seem to care about anything but the Circle-L—its cattle, its horses, its owners. So emotionless most of the time, he had demonstrated a

193

deep-seated devotion when he came off his horse and laid into Thrall.

Monte doubted that Farrell's dedication consisted of the kind of adoration that he himself had felt for Dora. Farrell would never have consciously hoped to have Dora for his own, or ever thought of Lurie as anything but his boss. That was how it had seemed, at least, when Farrell had been studying how to smash Thrall; he was defending his lady's honor, and incidentally his lord's domain.

It must have embarrassed him, afterward, to have shown that part of himself to a couple of other cowhands. He would probably see it as a weakness, a sign of lost control, to have let others see that he felt anything that strongly. It was safer to be hard-shelled and never show a crack.

It must have sickened his heart also to have anyone say out loud that a common cowhand had aspired to Dora's attention—and then to have had that same cowhand see him react. There was no telling how much Farrell would have known about Dora's past, but it wouldn't have mattered. At the heart of Farrell's code would be the assumption that nothing was ever a lady's fault. Monte had seen it, and Farrell had known he had let it be seen.

Although Farrell's display of private feeling had made a strong impression, it had not surprised Monte as much as Thrall had. For one thing, Monte had been surprised to see that Thrall was even more uncouth than he thought. For another, he was left to wonder where Thrall might ever have picked up the information that Monte had been infatuated with Dora. It was more than Thrall could have pumped out of Johnny Romaine even if he had had the chance. And it was a certainty he had never gotten it from anyone at the Circle-L.

It was hard to think of Thrall and not find him repugnant. On a very simple level he seemed to share a trait with Farrell: They both served their masters. But Thrall had chosen ugly ways to do what he was sent out to do. He was willing to bully a drunk or cheapen other people's feelings just to start a fight, and he didn't seem to care what came out of the fight.

Monte agreed with Thane. You couldn't blame Farrell. He had put himself on the line. And even if it had caused him the pain of embarrassment, Monte was sure he would do it again if he had to.

Chapter Thirteen

On Saturday, Thane had the boys clean and oil saddles. They set up their work in the cookhouse, which was warmer than the barn. Horace and Thane sat through an extra cup of coffee as the boys went to work on their first two saddles. Before long, the air was heavy with the smell of kerosene lamps, tobacco smoke, oil, leather, and breakfast residue.

"What would you think of crackin' that door?" asked Johnny.

Thane got up and opened the door about six inches. "Is that enough?"

"Maybe a little more," said Horace. "It's pretty thick in here."

Thane smiled as he relit his pipe. "It's those cigarettes Johnny smokes."

Johnny looked up and smiled. "How 'bout that

fella that took to sneezin' every time the room filled up with smoke? Remember him?"

"He didn't stay around long," Horace said. "I can't even remember his name, but it'll come to me."

Monte lifted the stirrup fender and swiped his oily rag across the saddle skirt below. "Was he a cowpuncher?"

"He was a bug-hunter," Horace answered. "He was interested in diggin' up old bones. He went off to another ranch up north."

Johnny spoke up. "His name was Sniffin."

"Aw, go on," Horace said. "I remember his name now. It was Edwards."

"Nice fellow," Thane offered. "Interesting to talk to. Educated. Shaved every day."

Horace nodded. "You meet all kinds."

After a little while, Thane went back to the house and Horace went into the kitchen to work. Johnny paused from scraping the underside of a wooden stirrup with his pocket knife.

"This is all right, isn't it?"

"Oh, yeah. It's almost like a day off."

Johnny's face lit up as he put on a clever smile. "Not quite," he said. "Not for me."

The next day was a real day off. The boys left the ranch in the morning, and Monte was sitting in the café before noon. Ramona said she might be able to close up the place for a little while in the afternoon so they could go out as they had planned.

At a little after one o'clock she said it looked as if

she could leave. She went back through the kitchen, presumably to her living quarters, for she came back out in a little while wearing a riding skirt and a pullover wool sweater. She carried her gray wool coat on her arm.

"You look nice," he said.

"Thank you." A faint blush came to her face as her eyes sparkled. She put on her coat and a pair of gray wool gloves, and she was ready to go.

As Monte walked her to the front door, she took a key from her pocket.

"I don't think I've ever seen you lock this door," he said as she turned to secure the door.

"I lock it every night, of course. But if I'm not going to be gone over an hour, I usually leave it open."

Monte gave her his hand as she stepped into the street. He thought of offering her his arm, but he remembered her comment that she felt as if someone was always watching. If she was self-conscious in this town, he did not want to make it worse at this point. They walked together to the livery stable, where Monte went to work getting the bay horse ready for the ride.

Although he had combed out the dark mane and tail pretty well on an earlier visit, it had been over a week and a half, and not all of the tangles came out the first time anyway. The horse stood patiently through the brushing and combing. After that, it let him pick up all four hooves for an inspection.

Ramona showed him where the saddle and bridle were stored, and he hauled them out. They were dry and dusty, but everything looked in order. The horse gave no trouble as Monte put on the saddle and then slipped the bridle over his ears and the bit into his mouth.

"Nice, gentle horse," he said.

"Got a heart of gold," she said with a smile.

Monte laughed. She must have heard it from Conde that day in the café. "You're kind of cute, aren't you?" he said.

She gave a little laugh. "If you think so."

Monte let Ramona go first as he led the horse through the stable and out into the street. "Are those stirrups adjusted for you?" he asked.

"Yes, they are."

He stopped the horse, flipped the reins into place with the ends curled around the saddle horn, and stood with his left hand on the swell of the saddle.

"Ready?"

"Ready."

She stepped forward and lifted her left foot toward the stirrup, but the toe of her boot missed the stirrup by an inch.

"Just a little more," he said. "Let me help you. Here, grab the saddle horn first."

She stood close to the horse, reached for the pommel, and raised her foot again. He cupped the back of her boot with his right hand and helped her find the stirrup. Then she pulled herself into the saddle with no trouble.

Her dark hair framed her face as she looked down at him and smiled. "Thanks."

"You're welcome," he said. "Let me get my horse, and we can be gone."

He had ridden the buckskin to town again, and

it stood at the hitching rail. He untied the horse, turned it into the street, and swung into the saddle. Ramona rode up next to him on the bay horse, and they were on their way.

They rode north of town, not speaking until the last buildings lay a quarter mile behind. It was a pleasant day. The air was cold, but the sun was shining and the wind was not blowing.

Ramona's dark hair hung loose and shiny as she rode on Monte's left. "It's nice to be able to get out," she said.

"I imagine it's been a while for you."

"I think the last time I went riding was in May, and I didn't go riding very much before that."

Monte remembered that her husband had been dead about a year and a half. She had probably been working just about every day since then. "How long have you lived in Eagle Spring?" he asked.

"Less than three years. A little more than two and a half."

"Oh. Uh-huh. I hope you don't mind my asking."

"No, not at all. We really don't know that much about each other."

"Well, my life's pretty simple. Grew up in Cheyenne. My folks died early. I went out on my own and worked. Spent some time down in Texas and New Mexico, then came back up here."

"And you've never been married?"

"Not even close. I guess you could say I had a bad case of puppy love, but that was a while back." He felt a small nag of conscience, but he thought the details would seem out of proportion if he went into them now. "Anyway," he said, "I've never been attached."

They rode on for a little ways until she spoke. "Well, as you know, I've been married. To Mr. Flynn."

She seemed willing to talk about the subject, so Monte went along. "What was your last name before you got married?"

"Morro. We have two last names, you know, but the one that matters is Morro."

"Oh, I see. And Mr. Flynn, where was he from?"

"He was from southern Colorado, like I was. We met in Colorado Springs."

"Did he have a business there too?"

"No, he had been a cook on a ranch, but he wanted to get married and have his own business."

Monte pictured the various cooks he had known. "He was a regular bunkhouse and chuck-wagon cook, then?"

"Yes." She looked over at Monte. "He was about your age or a little older."

Monte held back a smile as he looked at her. "And how old do you think that would be?"

She lifted her eyebrows. "Oh, about thirty. That's how old he was when I met him."

"So you married him, and then came up north here?"

"Yes." She had a serious look on her face now.

"How did you end up in Eagle Spring?"

Her face relaxed. "Well, he didn't have much money, and he wanted to find a town that didn't have a restaurant. He thought he could get started easier, so that's the way we did it."

Monte thought about how he might say something diplomatic. "It's too bad he didn't get to work at it a little longer. Startin' out on his own concern, and all, a fella would like to have gotten farther."

"Yes," she said. "We were here barely a year when he passed away."

"That's too bad." Monte thought for a second. "Haven't you ever thought about going back to Colorado?" Then he added quickly, "Not that I want you to, of course."

"Sometimes," she said, "but I don't think I'll go back for a while yet." She seemed to hesitate, but then continued. "You see, my family wanted me to marry another boy, and I didn't like him. So I married Mr. Flynn and left with him."

"Oh. And you think it would be kinda hard to go back and tell 'em it didn't last? It's not like things were all washed up because of something you did. I mean, if things didn't work out, it's not your fault." As soon as he spoke, he realized he might have said too much. It wasn't his business, and yet he wanted to stick up for her.

She gave him a slight frown as she shook her head. "You know how families are."

He wasn't sure that he did, but he said, "Uh-huh. Didn't they like Mr. Flynn?" He realized he didn't feel uncomfortable speaking the man's name.

"Oh, they never met him." She looked straight ahead and went on to say, "So when he passed away, I decided to go along on my own for a while. I thought I would just keep on with the business and see if I could make something out of it."

"Not to be pryin', but has it gone all right?"

She gave him a matter-of-fact look. "Just barely."

He hesitated and then asked, "Could you get out of it if you wanted?"

"I think so, if I wanted to sell it cheap. Mr. Wheeler has offered to buy it."

"For about a tenth of what it's worth?"

She laughed. "Maybe a little more than that."

They rode on for a few minutes without speaking. The sky was beginning to haze over, but Monte did not see anything to cause him worry. He looked over at the bay horse to see if it was sweating. Even a light exertion could warm up a horse that hadn't been ridden in a long while, and Monte didn't want the horse to overheat and then catch a chill. The horse looked fine, though, so he said nothing and rode on.

A little while later he saw a hill up to the left, and he thought it would give them a good view of the landscape.

"What do you think about riding up there?" he asked. "We could get a nice look at things."

She agreed, so they pointed the horses in that direction and let them climb the hill. It occurred to Monte that Ramona might want to get off and walk around, as she hadn't ridden for several months. He suggested it when they reached the top, and she said it was a good idea. He dismounted and stood by her horse as she let herself down. He felt a wave of emotion as he stood next to her under the open sky, with miles of country all around. He wanted to take her in his arms, but he did not want to risk spoiling their first time out together.

She must have felt something, too, for she gave

him a shy smile as she looked up through her eyelashes and said, "Thank you."

They walked slowly around the top of the hill, leading the horses and looking out over the wide plains. Off to the right lay the clump of buildings they had left behind, but otherwise there was nothing on the landscape but the land itself. Monte saw a few dots of cattle here and there, but he saw nothing that resembled a horse and rider.

After they had walked for several minutes, they sat down, each of them still holding a set of reins. She sat at his right, about a foot or so away.

He took a broad look at the country in front of them. "This really gives you a sense of being free, doesn't it?"

"Yes, it's so pretty."

He picked at the grass for a moment until he found the nerve to speak. "I was thinking about the other day when we were standing by the corral, and you said you always felt like someone was watching you."

She looked at him and nodded.

"I hope you don't feel that way here."

"No, not at all. Like you said, being up here lets you feel free."

He could not imagine putting his arm around her without being clumsy about it, given the way they were sitting and still holding the reins. But he wanted to kiss her, and he thought the moment was right. He looked at her, and her eyes met his. He set his right hand, with the reins, on the ground as he turned to her.

She turned to him, and their lips met. He felt a

current flow through him, and he knew he was kissing a real woman. He reached with his left hand and found her right elbow, then drew her closer as the kiss continued.

Then they were apart, and his eyes opened to her dark hair, dark eyes, and lovely face as she sat with him on this hilltop above the wide country, with the endless sky above them. His hand had moved from her elbow to touch her hand. He looked at their hands, his in a leather glove and hers in wool, and they seemed to belong together. His eyes met hers once again, and her face relaxed into a smile.

He moved toward her and kissed her again, briefly this time. "We ought to come here more often," he said with a nervous laugh.

She laughed also. "Yes, but if we came here every day, then everybody would know, and they wouldn't leave us alone." She moved her head in the direction of Eagle Spring.

He spoke without thinking. "Well, we'd just have to go somewhere else, then." When she didn't respond right away, he said, "That was just a joke."

Now her eyes met his. "It was a good joke."

He kissed her again, a short kiss like the second one, and then he drew away. He moved his right hand over to touch her left. They sat for a few minutes without speaking, and then he said, "I don't want you to think I'm in a hurry, but we probably ought to be getting back."

"No, I think you're right," she said, looking down at their hands. She looked up at him. "Thank you for taking me here."

"You're welcome."

Their hands came apart, and he helped her to her feet. They stood together for another long minute, and he could feel a chill that had set in as they had been sitting. He suggested they walk a ways before mounting up, so they walked to the bottom of the hill and out onto the plain. He checked the cinches on the horses and helped her into the saddle.

On the ride back, their talk came around to the weather and how unexpectedly a storm could come up. As a matter of course, Ramona said, "That's how my husband died."

"I had heard that," said Monte. It seemed as if she didn't mind talking about Flynn's death, so he went on. "But I didn't understand—or hear, anyway—how he came to be out in a blizzard if he had a business in town."

Ramona glanced at Monte and then back at the trail. She made the small frown he had seen before, and then she said, "He went out looking for a man who had disappeared."

"Someone here?"

"Yes. A man named Watkins."

Monte did not recognize the name. "How did he get himself lost? Did he live here?"

Ramona shook her head. "No, he was new here. He was around town for a few days. I think he was trying to get in good with Mr. Elswick."

Monte felt himself tense at the name, but he made himself focus on the topic of Watkins. "Was he a horse trader, or some kind of cattle buyer?"

"No, I don't think so. I think he had some information he thought Mr. Elswick would like."

"Oh, really?" Monte gave her a close look. "What kind of information?"

"About Mr. Lurie."

Monte made a quick reflection. It could have been about Lurie's dealings in the cattle business, or it could have had something to do with Dora. Or it could have had a little to do with both. "Did your husband, Mr. Flynn, know anything about the information itself—I mean, the details?"

She shook her head again. "I don't think so. My husband thought this man Mr. Watkins was some kind of a blackmailer. It seemed like he had gathered some information about Mr. Elswick and Mr. Lurie both and then was hoping to make the most of it."

Monte gave that a thought. There were certainly things in Elswick's past to be dredged up. "Sort of play one against the other, then, it sounds like."

"I guess so. Anyway, he went out on a ride and didn't come back. He didn't tell anyone where he was going, but my husband thought he was going to meet with Mr. Elswick. He didn't come back that night, so the next morning Mr. Flynn went out to look for him. Then the storm came up."

"A late-spring storm."

"Yes."

"Those can be hard even for people who know the country." Monte looked directly at her again. "Did you have any reason to suspect that your husband died from anything other than the weather?"

"No," she said, shaking her head more slowly this time. "There were no marks on him, and they found him with his saddle blanket wrapped around him

207

and a rope tied from his waist to the neck of his horse."

"And the horse was alive?"

"Yes."

Monte grimaced. "Well, that part doesn't sound so suspicious. But no one ever found this fellow Watkins?"

"No, not around here. He just seemed to disappear. Here in town, people seemed to think that Mr. Elswick told him to move on for his own health."

"He has a tendency to do that, but he also has a tendency to be somewhere in the background when a man turns up dead." Monte adjusted the slack in his reins. "What did this fellow Watkins look like?"

"Oh, pretty normal. A little rough, but not like a working man. He wore clothes that looked like they might have been nice at one time, but they were worn and needed cleaning. He had a beard, and he wasn't bad-looking."

An indistinct image loomed in Monte's mind. Something seemed familiar, but he couldn't be sure. "How about his eyes? What color were they?" He thought she would have noticed that.

Ramona's face brightened. "He had one brown eye and one blue eye."

Monte understood the glimmering picture now. The beard had thrown him off for a moment, but now he saw the man, spruced up and slicked down, coming out of a brothel. "I don't think his name was Watkins," he said. "I think it was Pryor."

It all fit together now. Pryor had come to blackmail Lurie or Elswick or both. That was probably where Thrall had picked up Monte's name in connection with Dora. Then he would have recognized Monte's name that first day out on the trail.

"Did you know him?" she asked.

"If it was Pryor, I knew who he was. I met him once. And he would have known something that would not have made Mrs. Lurie look good."

"Oh."

Monte looked around him at the landscape. He remembered what it had looked like from the top of the hill, and even better, from up in the foothills when he had gone hunting with Johnny. He had seen the whole rangeland south of Eagle Spring from that spot. He could imagine Pryor tucked away in some little nook. It would have been like Elswick to have someone of Pool's caliber—whoever he had had around at the time—to do away with Pryor, then have Thrall find a place to dispose of the body. That would have been a good job for Thrall—like a dog burying a bone. Somewhere out there, in the miles and miles of grass and sand and sagebrush, Pryor might be stashed.

"If it was Pryor," he said, "I would bet he rode out and never came back."

Her eyes were moist as she looked at Monte. "And Mr. Flynn died for nothing."

"It could be," Monte conceded.

"But he went out in good faith," she said, her voice quavering, "to help someone that he thought needed it." She wiped her eyes.

"That's a better way to think of it. He went out, and he got caught in a storm. It's hard to say it was anyone's fault."

She took a deep breath and seemed to be regaining her composure. "At the time, I thought it was like fate or destiny—like in the old stories, where north was the place of death. Now it seems like it was just an unnecessary mistake."

"It does, doesn't it?"

They rode along for a while without talking, until Monte thought of a question he had. "You said something that sort of struck me."

"What was that?" She blinked her eyes, as if she were coming back from her own wandering thoughts.

"About the old stories, about death being in the north."

"Oh, yes," she said. "Those were the old stories, before the Spanish came."

"Indian legends, then."

"Well, I guess so. But they're our stories, too."

"Oh, yeah. I didn't mean they weren't." He thought for a second and asked, "How far north would that have been, in those stories?"

"I don't know. Just north. I always understood it was in the ice and snow, but maybe down in Mexico it wasn't. Why?"

"Well, the Indians in the north here have their stories, too. One of 'em is about the giant that lives in the north."

She looked at him with a smile. "Really? That must be even farther north, then."

"I guess so. Down in Mexico, the U.S. is in the north. Then, in Texas and New Mexico, or even where you're from, up here is in the north." He motioned backward with his head. "But then there's still a lot of country from here to the Canada line, and prairies beyond that, and all the frozen country beyond that."

"Where the polar bears live," she said, smiling.

"Right," he answered with a nod and a wink. "And that's where I assume the real giant lives. We won't go there."

"Good," she said. Her face looked happy again.

Chapter Fourteen

On the ride back to the Three-Bar, Monte asked his young pal Johnny if he had heard of the fellow named Watkins.

"I don't recall," said Johnny, adjusting his hat.

"As I heard it, he was in town just before the big storm that Flynn died in."

Johnny lifted his head. "Oh, yeah. That's what got Flynn in trouble. He went out to look for him."

"Right." Monte went on to tell the story about Watkins as he had heard it from Ramona. He did not include his own interpretation that the man was Dora's first husband. Monte had appreciated Johnny's discretion in not including mention of Mrs. Lurie in his account of the fight between Farrell and Thrall; it was compatible with the assurance he himself had given Dora the first day he had seen her in Eagle Spring. And beyond that, his interpretation was only supposition anyway. Wrapping up the story, he said, "So there's a good chance no one ever saw him again."

"That sure makes sense. He just sort of faded out. That storm got everybody's attention, especially with someone dyin' in it, and since Watkins had passed through before that, I suppose no one gave it much thought." Johnny looked off to the rangeland on his left. "He might be out there somewhere."

The next morning, Thane told the boys he was planning to go to Denver to expedite the sheriff's return home. "If I go in person, he'll understand there's some real trouble brewing, not to mention a killing that no one has done anything about." Thane looked at each of the two ranch hands. "Horace is going to ride with me to Wheatland. He'll stay there for a few days and have himself a little holiday, while I go down and, I hope, bring back the sheriff. He'll have someone to travel back with, so that should be an encouragement." Thane paused and looked at each of the two boys again. "That means you're on your own. You know what to do. Keep your eye on things, and stay out of trouble, like always."

The boys nodded, then went out to get the horses ready for Thane and Horace. When the travelers were gone, they roped out their own horses and saddled up for the day's work.

The rest of the day turned out to be uneventful. The boys rode to the southeast, where nothing seemed out of the ordinary. They came back through the bad cactus area, and even there they found nothing needing attention.

The next day, Tuesday, they rode to the northeast. They saw more Circle-L cattle than they had seen a week or so earlier. Monte figured it was just a matter of where they rode and where the cattle were grazing. He thought of Farrell, and he wondered what action, if any, Lurie might be taking. Lurie would be the type to have brought in a stock detective by now—maybe someone recommended by his associates in Cheyenne.

At midday, after the two riders had finished their lunch and Johnny was done smoking his cigarette, he suggested a visit to the Riggs brothers' camp. "It'll be interestin' to know whether they heard anything about that fight between Farrell and Thrall," he said. "Besides, it's been a couple of weeks since we saw them boys."

They found the camp in the same place as before, but now it was a fur-trapping camp instead of a meat-hunting camp. George was skinning a coyote that he had hanging on the north side of the wagon, while Earl stood bent over at the tailgate, fleshing out a hide that was stretched on a wide board. Both brothers looked up, smiled, and said hello, but they did not stop their work. Monte and Johnny tied their horses to the front wheel of the wagon and walked over to a spot near the two brothers but not in their way.

"Hard at work, looks like," Johnny said as he and Johnny stood watching. "You been chummin' these coyotes in with your gut piles, George?"

The younger brother grinned. "It has helped. We've shot a couple that way."

"Are the hides good?"

"Oh, yeah. It's been cold long enough. They've got good fur."

Johnny turned to the older brother. "Well, how 'bout you, Earl? Keepin' busy?"

Earl nodded. "We shot these two this morning." He pointed with his knife. "That one on a gut pile. Haven't done too well with the traps yet, though." He raised his head and sniffed, and he had a serious look on his face as he spoke to Johnny. "I'm glad you came by. I thought I might have to ride over to see you, and I didn't want to have to leave George and all of this."

"Oh?" Johnny put both hands on his belt, above his woolly chaps. "Somethin' happen?"

Earl looked at Monte and Johnny both. "I think so. A person would have to do some lookin' to be sure, but I think Pool and Elswick did somethin' to our friend Conde."

Johnny's eyes widened. "Really?"

Earl looked around. "I don't want to shout it, you know. I've already told George."

Monte and Johnny moved in closer to stand by the wagon, between George and Earl.

"It happened yesterday," Earl began. "Along about evening, about four miles south of here and a little east. I was on a coyote stand, a pretty good little hidin' place, where I'd killed a nice coyote last year. I was sittin' there lookin' at nothin', when along come Elswick and Pool, with Conde in between 'em. They went on past me to the north a little ways, where there's some breaks and rough country. I thought I heard a pop, but I couldn't swear to it. Then a little while later they came out, just the two of 'em, without him. They had the horse with 'em, but I think they left him back in the breaks."

"You didn't go back there," Johnny said.

"Hell, no. When I was sure they were good and gone, I made tracks back to here. If he's out there, which I think he is, he's not goin' anywhere. Someone else can find him. I'll tell 'em where to look."

Monte looked at Johnny. "I don't think Thane can get back here any too soon with the sheriff."

Johnny had his mustache stretched down over his mouth as he shook his head. "I guess not." He looked at Earl. "I wonder what they had against Conde."

"I don't know. Not crooked enough, I guess." Earl glanced at his brother and then back at the other two men. "He came by here just the day before, on Sunday. He acted like always, but afterwards we thought he looked nervous. He said he wanted to get out, and he was goin' to try to draw what wages he had comin'."

"He probably stayed too long as it was," Monte said.

"Looks like it," Earl agreed. "Anyway, he said Elswick was out to get Lurie and Farrell and anyone else that got in the way." He looked at Monte. "Includin' you. Not meanin' any offense, but that's just what he told me. He said he didn't want to be around for any gunfight, so he was hopin' to pull out."

216

Monte felt a sense of dread setting in. "So you think they figured he came over here and talked too much?"

"I think so, even though he didn't say all that much."

Monte thought for a second. "Did he ever say anything about Weaver?"

Earl shook his head. "No, he didn't."

"Not even about the first part, when Johnny and I were there, and he came in with Thrall?"

"No, not a word."

"Did he tell you about the fight that Farrell and Thrall had last week?"

Earl nodded. "He said he wasn't there, but he told me it happened. He said Farrell beat the hell out of Thrall, and Elswick wanted to get even."

"Huh." Monte thought about that one. If Conde had never mentioned Weaver, then he might have felt implicated, at least by being present at the fight at Weaver's camp. He wouldn't snitch on Pool and Elswick if he thought he was in on it in some way, but he would tell about something he hoped to stay out of. Conde had to have known he was in with a crooked bunch, and he stayed on for the wages until he got scared. He was looking like a little bit of a coward, but it also looked as if he had his own principles about what he would say and what he wouldn't.

Monte looked at Earl. "They must have thought he knew too much and talked too much."

"It might be. They probably knew he came over here on Sunday."

Johnny spoke up. "And then, when he tried to

pull out, they decided to shut him up."

Earl spit off to the side. "It sure looks that way. It all looks like a crooked deal, and I don't think they should get away with it."

"They might not," Johnny said. "We'll just have to see."

Monte spoke again. "Back to this other point. You said Elswick was out to get someone, includin' me."

"Accordin' to Conde," Earl said in a definite tone. "He said Lurie and Farrell were the main ones, but your name was mentioned."

"Did he say how they were plannin' to do it?"

"Nope. He didn't go into any details. Maybe he didn't know any. I just think he wanted to get out."

"That's not very good news," said Johnny. "Not either part of it." He looked at George and then at Earl. "I hope you boys get to stay out of it."

"We do," Earl said. "That's one reason I didn't want to go back in there lookin' for him."

"It's just as well," Monte said. "And like you said, someone else can find him."

Johnny looked at Monte. "Well, I suppose we ought to move along and leave these boys to their work."

George spoke up from his skinning. "Did you already eat? We're gonna fix dinner as soon as we finish these two."

Monte felt his nose wrinkle. "We ate before we came over here, but thanks."

"You sure?" Earl offered.

"Oh, yeah," Johnny said, patting his stomach.

The Riggs brothers relented, and the visitors took

their leave. When they had ridden a good ways out of camp, Monte said, "I'm glad we already ate and didn't have to lie."

"Me, too," Johnny said. "I can castrate calves and sit right down and eat the fried oysters, but I don't like dead coyotes hangin' around the kitchen. And besides, I don't think we'd be doin' those boys a big favor by stayin' around their camp too long."

"I think you're right. We need to let them stay in the middle."

The boys rode west, and when they came to the main trail that led north to Eagle Spring, Johnny spoke up in an energetic voice.

"Say, we're not that far from town. What would you think of ridin' in? Nobody's waitin' for us at home, and you could see your girl."

Monte looked up the trail to his right. He had felt uneasy since the conversation at the Riggs brothers' camp, and he thought it might do him some good to take the edge off his nervousness. A visit with Ramona sounded like a good idea. "Sure," he said, "We can make a short trip."

The café was empty when he walked in and took off his hat. The bell on the door brought Ramona out of the kitchen, and Monte felt a wave of happiness at seeing her as she walked forward.

She showed surprise at seeing him. "Well, hello. I didn't expect to see you for another week. Is there something wrong?"

He thought he saw worry on her face. "Not really," he said. "We were just close to town, sort of, so we rode in."

"I'm glad you did." She looked behind him, at the

front door. "Come on back and sit down," she said.

He followed her to the back table on the left, where he most often sat. Instead of offering coffee and going to the kitchen, she sat down with him.

Their eyes met again, and he still thought he saw some worry. "Is there something wrong here?" he asked.

"I think so."

He glanced at the door and back at her. "Tell me about it."

She sat with her left hand on the table and her right hand in her lap. Her left hand moved as she spoke. "You remember the pretty piece of ivory you gave me, with the roses? Well, it's gone. I'm sure someone took it."

His eyes tensed. "Where was it?"

"It was in my room." She glanced toward the kitchen.

"Here in back?"

"Yes."

"When did it come up missing?"

"I didn't notice it until after we came back on Sunday."

Monte recalled her gloved hand turning the key in the door. "But you locked the place. Was the back door locked, too?"

"Oh, yes," she said. "I always keep it locked, unless I go out back."

He nodded. "But you leave the front door open when you go out that way. Did you go out on Sunday?"

"Yes," she answered. "I've thought back on it a

hundred times now. I went out once on Sunday and twice on Saturday."

"And the last time you saw the little piece of ivory?"

"I think it was Saturday, but I'm not sure. I don't remember seeing it early in the day on Sunday, but I looked for it after you left. That's when I noticed it was gone."

Monte squinted his eyes as he shook his head. "Someone went through your room, and it had to be planned. Did you ever have anything missing before?"

"No," she said. "I've thought of that, too. If someone wanted to steal something before, they would have taken Mr. Flynn's rifle."

Monte blinked. "That's true." He glanced at the door again. "Did you see any of Elswick's men in town on either of those two days?"

She took a deep breath and let it out. "I think so. I think I saw the longhaired one on Sunday, before you came. But I don't remember. Sometimes when I'm busy I see people out on the street, but I don't remember every person every day. I might have seen him on Saturday."

"Have you asked around to see if anyone saw anything while you were out on Sunday?"

"Yes, and of course nobody saw anything, but they knew I was out."

"Naturally. Whoever did it made short work of it. If I had to guess, I'd pick either Pool or Thrall. I think Thrall might have more for a motive, if he already made a move toward you, and he and I had a little run-in on our own. I don't know how to

221

second-guess him. I've been wrong about him before." Monte twisted his mouth and went on. "I
don't know. It could be either of 'em, or someone
we don't even know."

"Well, it has me worried."

"With good reason. Someone invaded your privacy." He put his left hand on hers. "Try not to
worry, though. Whoever took it had a reason, and
they might want to use that piece of ivory for something. We might see it again."

"I hope so. The roses mean more to me than they
could to anyone else."

He glanced at the door and then kissed her
quickly on the cheek. Patting her hand, he said,
"We just have to wait and see."

Johnny came into the café after a short while.
Things did not seem to have gone well for him, either. He was not smiling, and he had whiskey on
his breath. Monte thought it was probably time to
go, so when two other men came in and took a table
in the middle, Monte said good-bye to Ramona.
Without having had even a cup of coffee, he and
Johnny left.

Out on the trail, Johnny made an oblique remark
that he had not found his girl available. Then he fell
into a sulk, leaving Monte to his own thoughts.

It was disturbing to think that someone would
have gone into Ramona's living quarters. It wasn't
just a matter of theft, although someone had taken
something that obviously had personal value. More
than that, as he had said to her, someone had invaded her privacy. Someone had crossed the line
into her personal domain; it amounted to a kind of

violation of her boundaries as a person.

Monte's sense of Ramona included her physical presence. She was flesh and blood, with everything that made a woman. He had had an awareness, not clearly announced to himself, that his interest in her was conditioned by the knowledge that she was a mature woman. She had been married, which meant that she had known intimate feelings and sensations. She carried that maturity well, in a healthy, respectable way, and he had responded to it in a way that he felt was normal and honest. From the first time he kissed her, he knew he was not feeling the helpless swoon of puppy love. It was a grown-up feeling, not lust but a complex attraction to a woman who had physical presence. Other men would have sensed that quality in her, and the person who had stolen the ivory token must have known, if only intuitively, that it was an act against her physical person. The thief might also have known, or guessed, that stealing the piece of ivory was a way of sneering at the attraction that she and Monte were forming.

The theft of the ivory connected with what he had heard from Earl Riggs. Elswick was getting ready to make a move against him, for a variety of reasons that intersected. The most obvious reason was that he worked for Thane, sided with Lurie and Farrell, and had humiliated Thrall once by beating him up and once by watching Farrell do it. He was also showing interest in Ramona, which at the very least would spark some resentment in Thrall. It might also cause Elswick to think Monte knew more than he did about Elswick's shame in compromising a woman. If there was more to know, Elswick might think Monte had heard some of it through Ramona, who would have heard it from Watkins. Despite Elswick's effrontery, he had to have some sense of shame. It certainly seemed that way, with Weaver coming to grief so quickly and Watkins disappearing.

Watkins. Monte pictured him again as Ramona had described him, and he looked very much like Pryor with the polish worn off. It was more than a good bet that he was out in the rangeland somewhere, buried with his clothes on and with a bullet hole in his head or chest.

Looping back again to what he had heard from Riggs, Monte thought about Elswick's plan to move against Lurie again. Theirs was a fight over property and territory, as Monte had understood it before. Elswick wanted more power and control, while Lurie didn't want to yield. He had sent out Weaver and lost. Then he had sent out his best fighting dog and won. Now Elswick wanted to take it to another level.

It was hard to sympathize very much with Lurie. He wanted to protect his own power, but he wanted to send out others to do it. Monte had sensed something in the very fiber of the man that said it was morally acceptable for men to die over property. But even though Monte couldn't find Lurie admirable, he saw Elswick as worse.

Monte saw that he could get out of the way and leave Lurie with his own problem, but that didn't seem right. It wasn't just a matter of working for Thane, who sided with Lurie. Monte remembered the day he had seen Lurie swing little Claire up into the ranch wagon. Even if Lurie was the type who could condone bloodshed over a few hundred head of slobbering cattle, as Monte had imagined it earlier, he did have a family. It was real. Seeing the little golden-haired girl had made Monte see it and feel it more strongly than seeing Dora answer the door at the Circle-L ranch. Even if Monte didn't like Lurie, he believed that some of the man's motives were clean and deserved support.

He realized that it seemed more plausible now than before to think of Dora as Lurie's wife. He could accept it, whereas he could not consider her marriage to Pryor as anything but absurd. Dora was Mrs. Lurie; he had called her that with no second thought in his conversation with Ramona. Now he realized he did not resent Lurie on that score. Nor was he taking sides with Lurie because of any lingering adoration for the woman he couldn't have. As he looked into himself, he recognized that he didn't want her anymore, had not wanted her for quite a while. Somewhere along the way, he had forgiven her.

He knew it was important to be thinking these things through, to be reading his own emotions as clearly as he could. If he was going to stick up for Lurie, it had to be for the right reasons. In this case, it wasn't personal. Elswick was getting ready to make a move, and someone had to go up against him. Elswick had already gotten away with murder twice, as Monte saw it, and probably three times.

That was the deeper reason, he felt. If he knew something crooked was about to go through, he couldn't stand by and let it happen—not even if it happened to someone like Lurie, who didn't command much admiration.

Monte looked around and saw the country spread out in every direction. It was a wonderful country, free and open, as he and Ramona had appreciated it a couple of days earlier on their hilltop. He thought now of Ramona as he had seen her the most—shapely and graceful, smiling and radiant. He knew there was a possibility that he might not see her again, that he might not see any of this again. But he felt he had his mind clear on it. Come another sunrise or just the long night, he was going to put himself on the line. That was the way he was going to have to do it.

Chapter Fifteen

A cold blue wind came from the north. Monte hurried to the bunkhouse in the first gray light of morning, one hand on his hat and the other tucked against an armload of firewood. He pushed open the door of the cookhouse, rushed in, and slammed the door behind him. The smell of coffee and fried meat and potatoes mingled with the smell of wood smoke and kerosene fumes. Johnny stood at the cookstove, smiling as he turned to look.

"Cool out there?"

"Somewhat." Monte dropped the wood into the woodbox and pulled off his gloves. The air inside felt much warmer than it had before he went out. He took off his coat and hat.

He was glad to see Johnny in a good mood. The young cowpuncher had fallen into an unusual gloom the evening before, but he seemed to have slept it off. He was poking at the beefsteak with a long-handled, two-tined fork, and his face wore a pleasant expression appropriate to the occasion.

"Do we want to ride out in the wind?" Johnny asked.

"It's not all that strong, but it's cold. We can see what we think after breakfast."

The boys set the two skillets on the table and served themselves directly from the hot, sputtering cast iron. As Johnny salted down his beefsteak, he said, "I imagine the Old Man is in Denver now. He might even be on the way back, if he twisted the sheriff's arm just right."

"Well, I hope so," Monte said. "And I hope Horace is enjoying his days off in Wheatland."

The boys took their time at breakfast, putting away all the food Johnny had fixed up and drinking a few cups of coffee. The bacon grease in the skillets had solidified, and Johnny was smoking his second cigarette, when hoofbeats sounded in the yard outside.

Monte went to the door, remembering where he and Johnny had put the rifles the evening before when they had brought them into the bunkhouse. He looked out into the bleak daylight and saw two riders coming into the ranch yard. The rising sun cast them both in shadows, but he recognized the forms of Lurie and Farrell.

The riders came to a stop in front of the cookhouse. Lurie's voice came out of the bulky form. "Is Thane there?"

"No, he's gone. But come on in out of the wind."

Monte looked aside to tell Johnny who it was.

Then he waited at the door as both riders dismounted and tied up their horses. He held the door open for them as they came in, Lurie first and his hired man following.

They all said good morning. Johnny told the visitors to sit down while he rustled them some coffee. Lurie and Farrell sat down, but they did not take off their hats and coats. Monte noticed that their faces were flushed, as well they might be after riding in the cold wind.

"Where's Thane?" Lurie asked.

Johnny, with his cigarette in his mouth, set down two coffee cups and poured them full. "He's gone. He went to Denver to see about fetchin' the sheriff. I don't expect him back till tomorrow night or Friday, at the earliest."

"That's a hell of a note," said Lurie.

"Somethin' come up?" Johnny asked.

"Elswick wants to have a meeting. Tomorrow, at two o'clock. Out on Horsehead Flat."

Monte placed it in his mind. It was south of Weaver's camp and west of the main trail to town, about midway between Lurie's ranch and Elswick's.

"Is that right?" said Johnny. "Did he send a messenger?"

Lurie took off his coat now. "He left a note in the bunkhouse door. Farrell found it first thing this morning."

The boys looked at Farrell, who was taking off his coat and did not look up. They turned back at Lurie, who said, "We figured they left it there so they wouldn't have to go in any further. Whoever it

229

was, probably came in on foot while someone else waited."

"Uh-huh." Johnny stubbed out his cigarette in the flattened can. "You figure on goin', then?"

Monte could feel tension in the air. He thought Johnny might be a little too breezy for Lurie, who had come to speak with the boss. Lurie seemed irritated, and his face looked jowly as he spoke.

"I came down here first thing this morning to find out if I had someone to back me up."

Johnny didn't seem ruffled. "Well, the Old Man's gone. If you want us to, I suppose we can ride along. Don't you think, Monte?"

"I think Thane would want us to."

Lurie seemed a little calmer now. He gave the Three-Bar boys a look he might give his own men—a straight, confidential look with the clear blue eyes. "Why don't we meet a little west of there, then, about an hour earlier."

Farrell's dry voice came out. "There's a bluff about a mile west of there, where the cattle get out of the wind. It's an easy place to pick out."

Lurie glanced at him, then back at Johnny and Monte. "We can meet there, then."

A nod of assent went around the table.

Johnny rose in his seat and reached for the coffeepot. "I'll make some more of this," he said.

Lurie's voice was curt. "Not for us. We've got to go back."

"I'll make some anyway," Johnny said. He took the coffeepot to the kitchen and rattled around for a couple of minutes.

The visitors finished their coffee and stood up.

Lurie thanked the boys for the coffee, and Farrell muttered thanks as well. Then they put on their coats and were gone.

The wind picked up stronger in the middle of the morning and blew hard all day. The boys decided not to ride out. They took care of the horses, tidied up the bunkhouse, washed clothes, and draped the wash on chairs in the eating area. At dusk the wind died down a little, but then it picked up again after dark and howled all night.

In the morning it had quieted down, but it still cut a chill into Monte as he went out for firewood. He looked at the sky in the east and saw low, thin clouds in the gray sky.

The boys had breakfast, did chores, and loafed around awhile until it was time to saddle up and ride. The wind was cold but not forceful as they rode out of the ranch yard. Monte took a look at the ranch buildings, then turned his face into the wind and tipped his hat.

They arrived at the bluff well ahead of time. It was easy to find, as Farrell had said. It faced south, so it provided a sunny windbreak at this time of year. Half a dozen Circle-L Herefords got up and lumbered away as the Three-Bar riders approached the base of the bluff. The two riders dismounted in the bare, worn area and stood with their faces to the sun.

Monte had felt a nervousness in his stomach since the morning before, and it wasn't getting any better. He tried not to fret himself too much by wondering what Elswick might try, but he was sure Pool would be there and for a purpose. Thrall

231

would probably be on hand as well. Monte didn't think of Thrall as very much of a gunman, but he planned to keep an eye on him all the same.

Johnny had rolled a cigarette, smoked it, and fidgeted a while longer when Lurie and Farrell appeared in the west. As they rode nearer, Monte saw that they were dressed as usual—Lurie in brown and Farrell in denims—and that they each had a rifle stock poking forward on the left side.

Lurie spoke as they brought their horses into the shelter of the bluff. "We're a little early, but I'd just as soon get there first."

Monte and Johnny nodded and climbed onto their horses, then followed the other two riders out into the wind.

A mile later, they came to Horsehead Flat. Someone must have found a horse head there at some time in the past, but there was no such detail to distinguish it at the present. It was a flat, grassy area about a half mile across, with a few tufts of silver-green sagebrush waving above the pale grass. The wind was down to a breeze now but still cold.

The four men dismounted. Lurie pulled out his rifle, and Farrell did likewise. "Might as well be ready," Lurie said.

Monte and Johnny pulled out their rifles. Monte didn't like the feeling of taking that much initiative, but he realized that gunfire could scatter the horses and leave him on foot with no rifle.

Before long, three riders came over a hill in the east. Monte's stomach tightened as he recognized Elswick on the right, Pool on the left, and Thrall in the middle behind the other two. As the riders came closer they spread out about ten yards apart, with Thrall still lagging a few yards behind.

"Let's get spread out, too," Lurie said.

Farrell let go of his horse and moved off to the left. Lurie stayed where he was, with his horse close by. Monte walked a few yards to the right with his horse, and Johnny moved out to the far right.

The three riders stopped about forty yards away. "Looks like you brought help," Elswick called out, "but that's all right." The three men came in a little closer and dismounted; Thrall took the reins of the other horses as he held on to his own. Pool stood off to the side with his coat open.

Elswick had his dark coat buttoned up, with his pistol out of sight. "You can put your guns away," he said.

"That's all right," Lurie called back. "Let's hear what's on your mind."

Elswick pointed at Farrell as he looked at Lurie. "Your man there," he began, "attacked one of mine the other day. Laid into him without warning and wouldn't quit."

"Maybe he had reason," Lurie said.

"Maybe he thinks he did," Elswick snapped back. "And maybe he can answer to me for it. On the same terms."

Elswick took off his coat and laid it on the ground, set his pistol on top of it, and dropped his high-crowned black hat on top of that. When he turned back to face the others, Monte saw that he had a full head of hair, dark and trimmed and neatly combed. He was not wearing a vest as he had the other times Monte had seen him. The man looked like he was in good shape, but Monte questioned his judgment in wanting to fight a man who had trounced Thrall.

Monte looked across at Farrell, who turned and put his rifle in his scabbard. Then he took off the denim coat, laid it on the ground, and dropped his six-gun and light brown hat on top of it. As he stepped forward, Monte saw that he was wearing a common work shirt and not the more expensive one with two pockets.

Farrell walked up and stood in front of Elswick, who came around with a lightning left punch that knocked Farrell sideways and brought up his guard. The fight was on. The men squared off like boxers and then came together, trading punches until Farrell stepped back.

It occurred to Monte that Farrell might have less drive than he had had in the earlier fight. He might not feel as justified. Nevertheless, he stepped back in and traded punches again. Elswick put up a good fight, but Farrell rocked his head with a couple of solid punches and then gave him two in the midsection. Elswick backed off, came in swinging, and went into a clinch. From there he slipped his left arm up and around Farrell's neck and tumbled him to the ground.

Elswick was not trying to hit Farrell anymore, and Monte could not see the object of Elswick's maneuver until the men rolled over. Farrell had both hands on Elswick's right wrist, and a short gun barrel pointed upward. It was what some men called a hideout gun, and Elswick had gone for it.

Farrell twisted the wrist outward, then snatched

the gun with his left hand and backhanded Elswick with his right. He backed off and stood up, then stepped back.

Monte was surprised. Elswick had shown himself as a cheat, and rather early in the game. He had done it in public view, so it was something he would have to live with.

Then Monte's glance shifted, and he saw Pool raising his hand slowly and starting to lift his gun from its holster. This might be the setup, he thought—pull a gun on Farrell, and if he got it into his hand, let Pool have an excuse to draw down on him.

Monte levered in a shell and raised the tip of the rifle as he hollered, "Hold it, Pool!"

Everyone turned and looked at Pool. His dark snake eyes flickered, and he eased his gun back into its holster.

Monte let the hammer forward on his rifle and lowered the barrel. Then he realized his mistake. Time seemed to slow down as Pool's hand came back up with the six-gun, and Monte knew he couldn't get the rifle back up and the hammer cocked in time. He thought of Ramona, and his buckskin horse, and Ramona again with her long dark hair and sparkling eyes—and Pool's gun was up and out as Monte was bringing up the rifle. A shot rang out in front of him, and Pool turned.

Farrell had fired a shot with the little gun, Elswick's hideout gun. It had stung Pool, who was now making a chicken wing with his left arm as he twisted, writhing, and brought his dark six-gun around to point at Farrell.

Monte had his rifle up now and was cocking the hammer when a rifle boomed on his left. Pool's hat flew off as he sprawled backward, tipping his pale forehead and dark forelock to the sky.

Lurie had fired. He had stepped back a pace or two during the fistfight, and he had been outside of the triangle formed by Pool and Farrell and Monte.

Horses were running away, but everything was silent and dead-still in the circle of men. Pool was laid out on the ground, his pistol at his feet. Lurie was bringing the rifle down from his shoulder.

Monte looked at Lurie. He had been hanging back and letting his dog do the dirty work, but he was ready all the same. When Pool's aim had moved from Monte to Farrell, the owner of the Circle-L had pulled the trigger.

Lurie's voice came out clear. "Anyone here can vouch that I was justified."

The focus of attention shifted to Elswick, who was getting up off the ground. He stalled for a long moment as he stood there, and then he nodded. "Pool was a killer," he said, "even when I told him not to." He looked at Lurie. "He went to Weaver's camp on his own. You can ask Thrall."

"Or Conde." Monte heard his own voice and felt his blood racing. He took a breath to calm himself, then spoke again. "You can tell that to the sheriff. As you may know, he's on his way back. He'll want to talk to you and Thrall, and anyone who can tell him where to look for Conde. And someone can."

Elswick didn't flinch. He had had too much practice, and Pool couldn't say a word to contradict him.

Silence hung for a long moment. Monte glanced at Pool, whose body hadn't moved since it hit the ground. Elswick must have had a lot of confidence in Pool, to be willing to get into a fistfight and draw in Lurie or Monte, so Pool could clean up. Pool might have been able to do the job if Farrell hadn't been so handy with the little gun.

Monte eased the hammer forward again on his rifle. He felt himself settling down now. It had seemed as if things were over too soon when Farrell took the gun from Elswick, but it looked like the big fight was over now. Elswick's hole card was faceup, and Lurie's side had him well outnumbered. Even Farrell was armed now, as he stood a few yards away with the little gun in his hand.

Still, there was a loose end somewhere. Then it came to Monte, the image of a small ivory token with a dark etching of roses. He looked at Pool, and he was sure the dead gunman had it. Monte wanted it back, but he didn't want to have to search Pool.

"There's one thing," he said out loud. As all eyes turned on him, he looked at Elswick and said, "It's a piece of ivory, a little bigger than a silver dollar. If I don't get it back, I'm going to have to press for it."

Elswick's mouth was tight, the mustache firm, as he stared back. His face barely moved as he said, "Thrall has it."

Monte turned to Thrall, who had let the horses loose and now stood with his coat drawn back and his right hand hovering over his gun.

Thrall's gravelly voice floated across the flat. "Come and get it."

Ah-hah, Monte thought. They must have had this game worked out. But it would be hard to play it without Pool.

Monte cocked his rifle and said, "Show it."

Thrall looked at Elswick and lowered his hand. "Pool has it."

Now Elswick spoke. "Pool said he took it from a crib girl."

Monte eased the hammer forward again, then walked over and handed the rifle to Farrell. He stopped in front of Elswick. "You know that's not true," he said. "Admit it, or we'll see what happens."

Elswick gave a slight toss to his head and said, "It's not true."

Monte was irritated at himself. He wanted to make Elswick admit that he himself had lied, but with his light tone, Elswick could just as well have been saying that Pool had lied. But he had said what Monte had told him to say, so that would have to do. Monte took a breath and said, "Now let's have the piece of ivory."

Elswick turned, looked at Thrall, and made a motion with his head. Thrall walked over to Pool's body, stooped, rummaged for a minute, and stood up with a small, bright object in his hand. He walked halfway back to Monte and tossed it in the air.

Monte caught it with his left hand, and after being sure of Thrall, he looked at it. It was Ramona's gift, all right, back in his hands.

Monte looked at Elswick, who had his chin lifted again as he stood hatless in the pale sunlight. Monte wished he could punish the man more. Elswick had shown himself to be a cheat, and he had had to eat his own words, but a little shame wasn't much punishment for him. For as much as Monte was sure the man deserved more, he knew it wasn't his place to do it. Someone else needed to get the proof and deliver the punishment, and it was going to be hard for anyone to get complete knowledge. Elswick might have hired someone to kill Pryor, and Pool probably did pull the trigger on Weaver and Conde. Elswick did his best to keep his hands clean, and now he would blame it all on Pool, who couldn't say a word otherwise. It would have to be up to the sheriff and a reliable witness like Riggs.

Monte looked Elswick in the face. "You're the only one who knows for sure what you did and didn't do, here and elsewhere. That will stay with you."

Elswick's face was still hard. "I never touched that piece of ivory."

Monte felt a flare of anger. Elswick was trying to reduce his meaning to just the ivory. "You know I mean more than that," he said.

He turned and walked away, pausing to accept his rifle from Farrell, whose washed-out blue eyes showed no more expression than usual. "Thanks," Monte said. He looked around and found Johnny, who was waiting with his rifle barrel resting across his shoulder.

The two of them set off on foot to the southwest to catch the horses, which were grazing about a half-mile away and dragging the reins on the ground. When the boys had almost reached the horses, Monte looked around and saw Elswick with his hat and coat on now, standing with his back to Pool as Thrall went east after their horses.

"It just galls me that we can't do any more to him," Monte said. "After all the crooked things he's pulled."

"Lurie came close," Johnny said.

Monte looked back and saw Lurie and Farrell trudging northwest toward their horses. "It would have been his part, if anyone's, but it wouldn't have been right. He did what he could get away with."

Johnny spit on the ground. "Well, Elswick's game is up now, anyways. He's got plenty to worry about. I think you cut him pretty good with that remark about Conde."

Monte took a last look at Elswick. "That might be the one thing that'll get him."

Chapter Sixteen

Thane arrived that night at the ranch. He said he had spent nearly the whole four days in the saddle or on the train, and he looked tired. When the boys asked him where Horace was, he said Horace had ridden into town with the sheriff and would come home in the morning. Thane listened to the story of the fight on Horsehead Flat and shook his head. Then he said good night and went to the house.

Monte was surprised to see Horace cooking breakfast in the morning, but the cook just laughed. He said a roundup cook was used to getting up at three o'clock in the morning, so it was nothing to him to have gotten up later than that.

Thane came in looking better rested than he had the night before. After breakfast he picked up the conversation where it had been left off. He asked what had become of Pool's body, and the boys said they imagined Elswick and Thrall had taken it with them on the third horse.

"Well," he said, "maybe we should ride out there with the sheriff and give him a little support." He looked at Monte and Johnny.

"I've been thinkin' it over," Monte said, "and I think maybe I've done enough. Or at least as much as I can. I've been here a full month, so maybe it's a good time to call it even."

Thane gave him a look of surprise. "You mean you want to quit?"

"I'd like to go to town to check on something first. As for this other business, I just don't think there's anything else I can do. It's in the sheriff's hands, and Johnny can give him any information he needs."

Thane looked at Johnny, who nodded. Then he looked back at Monte. "Don't do anything in a hurry. We'll be back this afternoon or evening, and we can settle up then if you want to."

Monte agreed to that. Thane and Johnny finished their smokes and got ready to go to town. Monte said he would go in later. He went to the bunkhouse and sorted out his gear so it would be ready. He knew it was time to move on, but he wanted to talk to Ramona first.

On his way into town, he looked around him once more at the spreading country. He was glad to be able to see it and take it all in, but it also crossed his mind once again that Pryor might be out there somewhere. If he was, and even if no one ever found him, the fact would always be there. Elswick could lie about Weaver, and he could try lying about Conde. But there was such a thing as truth. Monte believed there was a superior knowledge, a view from above that was bigger than any one person. Some punchers related it to judgment and called it the big tally book. Whether there was a mind to manage it he didn't know, but he believed in an absolute truth.

As for Elswick, his game was no doubt up, as Johnny had said. He would have the sheriff asking questions, and even if he didn't get brought to justice, people would have him under scrutiny for a long while to come. Monte thought there was a chance that Elswick would try something to get even, but he was probably busy trying to cover his own tracks.

As Monte rode into Eagle Spring, he thought a couple of people gave him a look, but he couldn't be sure. He thought he might be feeling self-conscious, knowing that there had been a gunfight and he had been present. When he walked into the café, three men who sat at a table talking looked up at him; then they went back to their conversation.

Monte set his hat on the table in back, but he did not sit down. Ramona stood facing him, her hands together but not still.

"I heard there was trouble," she said.

"It's mostly over." He looked at her eyes and saw worry.

"The sheriff went out with Mr. Thane and your friend Johnny, and two other men."

He nodded. "I knew that a few of 'em were going out. I could have gone, but I didn't." He tried to put on a smile, but it did not come easy yet. He reached into his left coat pocket, put his hand around the ivory token, and brought it out for her to see.

She gave a cry of surprise, and the men at the table looked around. When they turned back to their conversation, she said, "You found it. Who had it?"

He hesitated for a second. "Pool did."

Her eyes searched his. "But you didn't shoot him. I heard Mr. Lurie did."

"He did. I got it back after that." He held it toward her, and his voice softened as his feelings did. "Here. Take it. It's yours."

She held out her right hand, and he laid the piece of ivory in her palm.

"Thank you," she said.

"You're welcome, Ramona."

She touched the dark etching with the tip of her left index finger, then raised her eyes to look at him. "You're not happy," she said. "Is there something else?"

Better to get to the point, he thought. "Yes, there is. I'm thinking of quitting my job at the Three-Bar, and I wanted to ask you something first."

Her eyes were steady. "Go ahead."

"Well, I was wondering if you'd wait for me. I want to go see that place I told you about, off in the mountains. I could send for you, or I could come back for you."

Their hands met, both of his and both of hers.

"Until when?"

"Probably the spring."

"Will you come and see me before you leave, or are you going now?"

"I'll be back tomorrow. I haven't quit yet."

"All right," she said, giving his hands a squeeze. "Then you'll wait?"

"Yes, I'll wait."

Back at the ranch, Monte had all his gear ready to go and felt restless around the bunkhouse. He decided to go out and chop firewood to work off some of his impatience, and that took him till sundown. He did the evening chores of pitching hay to the horses and checking their water trough. Then he went in to sit at the table.

Thane and Johnny rode in after dark, so Monte put on his hat and coat and went out to help Johnny put away the horses. Monte lit a lantern in the barn, and after they had finished with the horses, Johnny sat on a sack of grain and took out his makin's.

"I suppose you'd like to hear the story," he said.

Monte shrugged. "Whatever there is of it."

Johnny rolled his cigarette and lit it. "We found Thrall with a bullet hole in him."

"Really? Where?"

"He was sittin' against the barn there at Elswick's."

"Was he dead?"

"No, he wasn't, but he wasn't goin' anywhere fast. He wanted to get to town to the doctor, but the sheriff got him to talk a little first."

Monte nodded for him to go on with the story.

"Well, it seems that when they got back from the flat, Elswick put him to work diggin' a hole in the barn. He wanted to go out and get Conde, and bring him back and bury him there, and put hay back on top of it all."

245

"Uh-huh."

"So Thrall dug the hole, and he got to thinkin' somethin' was suspicious when Elswick told him to dig it deeper."

Monte recalled the scene of Elswick watching Thrall daub the horse's hooves, and he remembered how it had reminded him of a big dog watching another dog dig. "Uh-huh."

"So they went out that night—last night. There's a pretty good moon right now. They went out and brought Conde back."

"The hell they did. Well, I guess he would've kept all right for a few days out in the cold weather."

"Well, they did, according to Thrall. They got Conde unloaded and got the horses put away, I guess. Then, when they were standin' at the edge of the pit, Elswick tried to put a bullet through Thrall's gizzard. Thrall had a shovel and hit him a pretty good lick, and then got the best of him, but he did get a bullet through the guts." Johnny pointed to his right side, just above his belt.

"Well," he went on, "Thrall wanted to get out of there, but he didn't have the strength to go saddle a horse, so he sat down out in the sun. It was mornin' by then."

Monte gave a low whistle. "So where was Conde?"

"In the hole. Elswick got Thrall to do everything up to that point."

"And where was Elswick?"

Johnny raised his eyebrows as he took a drag on his cigarette and exhaled. "Hangin' from a rafter at the end of Thrall's lariat."

Monte let out a heavy breath. "He should have saved that strength to catch a horse, but maybe he just wanted to make sure." After a moment's thought he said, "I guess Elswick didn't want anyone to ask Thrall, after all."

Johnny shook his head. "I guess not. But the sheriff's doin' just that, back in town now. They got Thrall patched up a little, and he doesn't like the bullet hole."

"I don't suppose he does. Well, who knows how much of the truth he'll tell."

"No tellin'. But he insists he never shot anyone."

"Maybe not. And from what Riggs says, he wasn't there when they took Conde out for a ride." Monte shook his head. "Whew. Now the sheriff doesn't have to go out and look for Conde."

Johnny held his cigarette sideways and looked at it. "No, he doesn't. Elswick brought in the evidence for him."

Monte thought for another moment. "Then there's still the possibility that he could find out something about Watkins."

"He's workin' on it, but Thrall is a harder nut to crack on that one."

Monte didn't answer. He waited for Johnny to finish his cigarette. Then he blew out the lantern and walked with Johnny to the bunkhouse. The moon was full and bright, and Monte could imagine Elswick and Thrall riding out to the breaks at night. Then he pictured Elswick hanging from a rafter. Something had caught up with him, but it was more retaliation than punishment. He wondered if, even still, justice had been served. Maybe

247

so. If Elswick hadn't committed his other crimes, he wouldn't have attempted the one he got caught at. Monte shook his head. He had done his part, anyway. He had put himself on the line when it mattered, and it was probably his comment that made Elswick anxious about Conde. That should be good enough.

The next morning, Monte drew his pay and took leave of the Three-Bar ranch. Thane shook his hand and told him he was welcome to come back anytime to work or just to stay awhile. Johnny walked with him outside for a few parting words.

"If you weren't in such a hurry to leave, we could go up and hunt elk as soon there's not so much of a moon."

Monte looked at him sideways. "Do you need to get another set of elk ivories, or do you just want me to stay around and help you build an icehouse?"

Johnny smiled. "I ain't sayin'. If you stuck around, you might find out."

Monte put out his hand. "Well, I'll have to wait till later, then. It's been good workin' with you, Johnny. So long."

Johnny put out his hand and shook. "So long, Monte, and thanks."

Monte climbed onto the buckskin horse, which he had already loaded with his bedroll and war bag. He touched his hand to his hat and rode away. He looked back once and waved again at Johnny, and then he was gone.

He rode the buckskin horse into Eagle Spring, where the frost still lay in the shade as he looked up and down the main street. Ramona came out of the café and stood on the sidewalk as he turned his horse in and dismounted. She stepped down from the sidewalk to stand beside him in the sunlight.

Her dark hair and dark eyes were shining. He would want to remember her like this, he thought.

"Well," he said, pointing his thumb at the bundles tied to his saddle, "I'm packed, as you can see."

She nodded, and she had a faint smile. "Are you in a hurry, or can you wait awhile?"

"Oh, I'm not in a hurry to leave you. I could wait a little while." He held out his hands, and she joined them with hers. "I hope you're not in a hurry for me to leave."

"No," she said, "but are you sure you want to leave alone?"

His heart beat faster as he looked into her eyes and realized what she had said. "You mean you might be able to go with me now? I hadn't dared to think you could just leave right out. Do you think you could?"

Her eyes were moist and shining as she nodded. "If you want me to."

He glanced at the building. "How about your business?"

"I can get away from it. Not at a good price, but I can get something for it."

He could feel himself trembling. "There's nothing I'd want more, Ramona. Believe me. But could you just leave?" He bit his lip. "We can find a judge somewhere along the way. In Douglas, or Casper."

"I trust you," she said. "I trusted Mr. Flynn."

He took her in his arms and kissed her, there in plain view in the main street of Eagle Spring. When they drew apart, he asked, "Why did you ask me if I could wait awhile?"

She blushed. "I have things almost ready, but I needed to be sure. And it will take you a little while to get my horse ready."

Later that morning they rode north out of Eagle Spring. As Monte explained to Ramona, they would go north a ways and then make a wide curve to the west. They would follow the trail toward the western mountains and a cabin near a place called Crowheart.

Coyote Trail

John D. Nesbitt

Travis Quinn doesn't have much luck picking his friends. He is fired from the last ranch he works on when a friend of his gets blacklisted for going behind the owner's back. Guilt by association sends Quinn looking for another job, too. He makes his way down the Powder River country until he runs into Miles Newman, who puts in a good word for him and gets him a job at the Lockhart Ranch. But Quinn doesn't know too much about Newman, and the more he learns, the less he likes. Pretty soon it starts to look like Quinn has picked the wrong friend again. And if the rumors about Newman are true, this friend might just get him killed.

___4671-7 $4.50 US/$5.50 CAN

Dorchester Publishing Co., Inc.
P.O. Box 6640
Wayne, PA 19087-8640

Please add $1.75 for shipping and handling for the first book and $.50 for each book thereafter. NY, NYC, and PA residents, please add appropriate sales tax. No cash, stamps, or C.O.D.s. All orders shipped within 6 weeks via postal service book rate. Canadian orders require $2.00 extra postage and must be paid in U.S. dollars through a U.S. banking facility.

Name_____
Address_____
City_____ State_____ Zip_____
I have enclosed $_____ in payment for the checked book(s).
Payment <u>must</u> accompany all orders. ❑ Please send a free catalog.
CHECK OUT OUR WEBSITE! www.dorchesterpub.com

GOLD
OF
CORTES
TIM McGUIRE

Amid the dust and desolation of southwest Texas lies a secret that has lasted for centuries—the hidden treasure of Aztec artifacts hoarded by Hernan Cortes. When Clay Cole finds English lord Nigel Apperson and Dr. Jane Reeves wandering the Texas desert, searching for the mythical prize, he agrees to sign on as their scout. Together they confront Texas Rangers, desperadoes, and the relentless Major Miles Perry, whose driving desire is to court-martial Cole for treason at Little Big Horn—treason Cole never committed. All that stands between them and the fortune of a lifetime is a Mexican revolutionary and renegade Comanches!

NEW HOPE

Ernest Haycox

New Hope combines three of Ernest Haycox's finest short novels with the interconnected stories he wrote about New Hope, a freighting town on the Missouri River in what was then Nebraska Territory. In "The Roaring Hour," Clay Travis, the new town marshal, and his fiancée, Gail, are up against the combined forces of the gambling hall owner, the sheriff controlled by him, and the local outlaw leader. A young upstart holds up a stagecoach in "The Kid from River Red" to prove his manhood and impress an outlaw. "The Hour of Fury" tells the tale of Dane Starr, who has come to town to lose his identity as a gunfighter and instead finds himself at the center of a dangerous power struggle.

___4721-7 $4.50 US/$5.50 CAN

Dorchester Publishing Co., Inc.
P.O. Box 6640
Wayne, PA 19087-8640

MAN WITHOUT MEDICINE

CYNTHIA HASELOFF

Daha-hen's name in Kiowa means Man Without Medicine. Before his people were forced to follow the peace road and live on a reservation, Daha-hen was one of the great Kiowa warriors of the plains, fabled for his talent as a horse thief. But now Daha-hen is fifty-three and lives quietly on the edge of the reservation raising horses. When unscrupulous white men run off his herd, the former horse thief finds himself in pursuit of his own horses and ready to make war against the men who took them. Accompanying him on his quest is Thomas Young Man, a young outcast of the Kiowa people. During the course of their journey, Daha-hen adopts Thomas and teaches him the ways of the Kiowa warrior. But can Daha-hen teach his young student enough to enable them both to survive their trek—and the fatal confrontation that waits at the end of it?

___4581-8 $4.50 US/$5.50 CAN